WESTGATE ELEMENTARY
LIC

JUNIOR DRAGSTER DREAMS

Always have a dream!
E.J. Carter
2013

JUNIOR
DRAGSTER DREAMS

HOW SAM FOUND HIS OWN RIDE

C.J. Carter

Greer Avenue Books
Blue Ridge, Georgia 30513

Greer Avenue Books
8658 Old Dial Road
Blue Ridge, Georgia 30513
706.838.4932

Published 2011
Printed in the United States of America
ISBN 0-9761692-2-3

Cover and book design by Margaret Johns, Sage Design, LLC

ACKNOWLEDGMENTS

I wasn't planning to write a book. I simply asked a former professional drag racer to tell me what it was like to travel a quarter of a mile in seven seconds at 200 miles per hour. His passion for the sport surprised me. One day, with no forethought whatsoever, I jotted down the plot to this book. Then I wrote it. Not only was that former racer's love for drag racing the inspiration for this story, Carl Fischer, Pro Stock No. 3183, also served as technical adviser. Without his experience as a drag racer and his knowledge of all things automotive, there would be no book.

Karen Mullinax and her family were invaluable. If Karen wasn't a cheerleader in high school, then she certainly should have been. Her enthusiasm is contagious. The entire Mullinax family: Karen; husband, Bobby; and son, Chase, took an afternoon to bring Chase's two dragsters to the Atlanta Dragway for the photo shoot that became the cover. Former junior racer Chase and junior racer Mackenzie Butler both took time to describe their drag racing experiences to me. Chase was the 2008 Atlanta Dragway Track Champion for thirteen to seventeen year olds, and Mackenzie was the 2008 Atlanta Dragway Track Champion for eight and nine year olds.

Three friends—Pat Potter, Suzanne Tarrant, and Kathleen Werneck—read the first draft, and Kathleen proofread the final version.

Roy Hill of Roy Hill's Drag Racing School explained to me how to safely drive a race car. Bob Eckert lent expertise regarding jukeboxes. Bradley and Melissa Shuford suggested some "kid talk."

William B. Hedgepeth edited the book. Linda Morse assisted with the title.

Crystal Wilson of the Atlanta Dragway connected me with sources. The management of the Atlanta Dragway allowed access to the drag strip for the cover photo shoot. Eric Lotz and Mario Hirose of the National Hot Rod Association spoke to me about various facets of drag racing and the NHRA. Rich Schaefer of the NHRA's Southeast Division office cleared up some confusion.

Mike Bos of Mike Bos Chassis Craft answered some technical questions.

JUNIOR
DRAGSTER DREAMS

HOW SAM FOUND HIS OWN RIDE

CHAPTER 1
Bully

Sam spit a wad of dirt from his mouth and dreaded what he'd see once he could stand up from where he'd just been knocked to the ground once again by Truman, the bully of his class—the bully of the whole neighborhood, in fact.

His upper arms were getting really sore where Truman, with his lips curled into a snarl, had punched him and kept punching him, punching him. But Sam now was putting everything he had into just keeping calm as he pushed himself up from the dirt and faced the rest of his classmates, all of them gathered round and staring at him. Just like yesterday and the day before.

"What!" he said defiantly, as he wiped his runny nose and walked away. He heard the other kids muttering. A few giggled.

Sam, his hair a tangled mess, figured his face was probably becoming as red as his hair because he could feel the warmth spreading up from his neck. He hated this uncontrollable tendency he had to blush, but when he was upset there was nothing he could do about it except to stand up as tall as he could and make himself calmly walk away—which is what he did.

Back home alone, Sam clomped up to his room and closed the door. Crawling into his secret hiding place in the back of his small narrow closet, he wanted to cry, but instead he just leaned against the wall, pulled his knees up into his chest, wrapped his arms around them, then let the hurt and shame take over. Most of the time, Sam felt as if he was missing something—as if he was missing out on something. But he could never quite figure out what that something was. It was like an odd hollow space inside. That's all he knew, but he knew he felt it.

Sam crouched in his private cubbyhole for quite awhile, trying not to think about Truman's snarling face or the heavy unhappiness that almost always seemed to hang over him. His mother wouldn't be home from work for an hour. By then, he thought, he could clean up and maybe she wouldn't notice either his mood or the new bruises Truman had left.

The doorbell chimed. Because his mother worked at Georgia Tech, it chimed the first nine notes of *Ramblin' Wreck from Georgia Tech.*

Sam ignored it.

It chimed again. And again. And again.

"Crap."

Sam crawled out of his closet. From his upstairs bedroom window, he could look down and just barely see whatever was outside the front door. The branches from a dogwood partially blocked his view, but he saw all he needed to see: red glasses, short spiky hair.

"Oh, no," Sam muttered under his breath. "Not Chloe."

"Sam," she yelled, "I know you're in there. Open up this door or I'll break the laundry room window again. Your mother will kill you. Let me in. I mean it."

There was no stopping her. Sam knew it.

He ran downstairs, saw the blurry shape of Chloe through the leaded glass window in the front door, opened it, and let her in. She went straight through the house to the black and white—very retro—kitchen and helped herself to Cheetos and Goldfish crackers.

"You'd better get cleaned up before your mom gets home," she chirped. "You don't want her calling the principal again. Do it. Now."

Chloe was so bossy.

But she was right. Sam ran back upstairs, washed his face in the single bathroom he shared with his mom, wiped the blood off his nose, pulled his hair down over the worst of the scratches. Then he returned to his closet and found a clean shirt. He chose one with long sleeves that could hide the bruises Truman had just made on his arms. Back downstairs, he found Chloe standing by the back door, tapping one pink-and-red polka-dot Converse sneaker on the floor.

"Come with me," Chloe ordered. "I need your help. I found a dog."

CHAPTER 2

Trunk

Sammy, I'm home."

"Sammy?"

Claire McCormick was relieved her son wasn't home. This was the date she dreaded every year. It was the anniversary—the sixth this year—of the day her husband, Sammy's father, died. The day weighed down on her almost as if she were wearing a bulletproof Kevlar vest—the same one Sammy's dad, Big Sam, wasn't wearing the day he was killed.

After going through the entire house to double-check that Sammy wasn't home, Claire finally walked down into the basement in the spirit of a serious ritual duty. At the bottom of the stairs, she paused, took several deep breaths, and turned on the light. As always, it was dim down there. She proceeded across the concrete floor to a little room in the back corner that stayed locked. Sammy had never been inside this room, had never even asked his mother about it—a fact for which Claire was grateful.

She selected a key from the ring of keys she had brought with her and unlocked the door. And there it was: The old antiqued orange chest she'd had since college. It was the only thing there was in the tiny room. Claire reached up and pulled the chain to turn on the light—a lone sixty-watt bulb hanging from the ceiling. As she did this, a cobweb caught her arm.

She brushed away the web then resumed her annual ritual. First, Claire recited a little prayer of thanks for all the glorious times she and Big Sam had shared together. Then, she reached behind the trunk to remove a single brick from the wall. Behind the brick was a small black velvet box, the one Sam handed her the night he proposed. Inside was her antique engagement ring. She took a moment to remember that night, pausing as her eyes welled with tears.

Finally, Claire removed the old skeleton key from the box. It was on a chain that also held Big Sam's dog tags. She unlocked the trunk. And now, as she slowly pushed back the lid of the trunk and heard the familiar creak of its rusty hinges, the memories flooded her. Claire pulled her blond hair up off her neck and took a few extra minutes to catch her breath before she could make herself dive into an ocean of unforgettable scenes from the past.

This pretty thirty-four-year-old widow, one by one, started to remove all the reminders of Sammy's dad that she had packed away six years ago. She remembered it had been no more than twenty minutes after the Casualty Assistance Officers—the Marines who came to deliver the news of her husband's death—left the house that she quickly began collecting and assembling all the memories and packing them away in this trunk, the same one that had seen her through college, early marriage, and now death. For six years, it had guarded the secrets she held sacred.

Sammy was only four when his father was killed. He remembered little of his dad, and that was the way Claire wanted to keep it at least when it came to that one thing. Sammy remembered his dad's kind spirit and the fact that Big Sam's hair was the same red color as his own. He remembered his dad was big and brave and was a Reserve Marine. Claire always told him what a good man his father was. Whenever Sammy would ask about him, she would always speak about Big Sam with loving fondness, but Sammy saw that it always seemed to make her sad so he didn't ask as many questions as he wanted to. So there was a lot about his father that still remained a mystery. Most of all, Claire didn't want Sammy to know of his dad's great passion, the one aspect of his life that made Claire live in fear that her son would also die.

Big Sam did die, but it turned out that his death had nothing to do with the thing he seemed to live for—and which had caused her so much fear.

But still, Claire worried that if Sammy knew about his father's dangerous pursuit, he would naturally want to try it, too. And she simply couldn't let that happen. So the trunk stayed locked and hidden, except for once a year, on this tearful anniversary of the passing of Big Sam.

Claire pulled out first one, then another once-shiny trophy. Still another. She ran her hands over each one, and she kissed the name inscribed on the small brass plate affixed to each: Sam McCormick Sr.

Next came the large manila envelope containing newspaper clippings. Claire took the time to read several articles about her husband and about his triumphs. Then she carefully lifted out the folded shirt with her husband's name on it. Next came his helmet, his fire suit, and his fire retardant shoes. She buried her face in his clothing as she did every year and breathed in the memories of the only man she had ever loved. And finally lost.

Sammy must never know. Never. She couldn't bear to lose him, too, and in her heart Claire knew she would if Sammy ever took up his dad's often dangerous avocation. She was thankful that he had never seemed all that interested in cars. Baseball would be good, Claire often thought. Or football. Anything, really, except cars.

When Claire suddenly heard voices outside—Sammy and Chloe were approaching the house—she rushed to put everything back into the trunk. *Click* went the lock as she turned the key. Back into the velvet box went the key, along with the dog tags. She removed the loose brick; placed the box behind it; replaced the brick.

Just as she let herself out of the little room and locked it, she heard Sammy and Chloe going into the garage.

Claire took another deep breath, shook out her hair, straightened herself up, and walked back up the stairs of this century-old house she and Big Sam bought in Atlanta's comfortable Virginia-Highland neighborhood—when they found out they were going to have a baby.

CHAPTER 3

Dog

H ere, Chloe, here's a box."

"What?"

"A box," Sam said. "What, are you deaf?"

"Sam, don't be stupid."

"Shut up. What are you talking about?"

"Sam, this dog is too big to stay in a box like this. After Truman's, we can go to my house. We've got some old blankets and pillows. Mom will never miss them. I'll sneak in and get them from the utility room. Then the puppy can just stay in the whole garage. He doesn't need a box. Your mom never comes out here. It'll be OK."

"But."

"Trust me on this," she nodded. "I have three dogs. He needs to be able to run around. And you'll need to check on him during the night. I'll help. We'll decide on times, and we'll take turns. We'll set our alarms and take turns feeding him and checking on him all during the night. Once every hour. It'll be easy for you to sneak out back. I'll climb out my window and come over here. Mom won't hear me. When she goes to sleep, she's out."

Earlier, Chloe had led Sam through their Atlanta neighborhood and over to a place called Callanwolde, a grand old mansion on Briarcliff Road, where, after school this afternoon, she had stumbled on a brown puppy. It was all alone, not another dog in sight. It was hiding in a hole and whimpered when Chloe fell almost right on top of it.

She nestled the little dog back into the hole, covered it with pine straw, and ran to get Sam.

Sam hadn't wanted to enter the grounds of Callanwolde because the two of them had been kicked out not long ago by the old caretaker. And it wasn't because they had damaged anything on the property. Chloe was playing hopscotch on the back patio, and Sam was shooting marbles when the creepy old man—he was always hunched over—found them and ran them off. He was a deaf mute, and they couldn't understand a word he said, but they got the point that day and hightailed it out of there.

Today was the first time they had returned. Callanwolde had a grim, spooky look about it, set back from the road and shrouded under massive old hardwoods. The place was huge, its exterior walls covered with ivy. Sam always thought it looked like the scene of a murder.

"Chloe, no. I'm not going there."

"Shut up," Chloe said, as she ducked through a hole in the fence behind the ninety-year-old structure that looked like the perfect setting for a scary movie. At one time, it was a private home owned by the Candlers, some bigwigs from The Coca-Cola Company, but today people used it for parties and weddings. And it looked like plans were in the making for some big shindig tonight. There was a lot of activity. All the lights were on. There were cars everywhere. They'd have to be careful.

Sam didn't want to, but he followed Chloe through the hole in the fence, then, in an instant, he fell to his knees. Before Chloe could say another word, Sam was hugging the puppy.

"My mom won't let me keep it," Chloe said. "We have too many dogs. You have to take it."

"Mom will kill me," Sam said, but he picked up the pup anyway and started walking back toward the hole in the fence.

"U ds ou ow," came the angry scream.

It was the old caretaker, running after them. He was bent forward, as usual. His nose looked more crooked than ever, and he was waving his bony hands in front of him. He probably felt right at home on Halloween. One thing was for sure, he didn't need a costume.

Chloe tripped. "SAAAM," she shrieked. "Help me!"

Sam looked back; the caretaker had her by the arms. He sure couldn't leave her with monster man. Sam went back.

"I ak ou ide. Om," the scarecrow man shouted.

"Let me go," Chloe said as she landed a kick on his shin. It was enough. He let go. Chloe, Sam, and the pup took off.

Just as Chloe ducked through the hole in the fence, right behind Sam, the caretaker grabbed her leg and off came her right sneaker, but she kept going.

They ran—well, Chloe limped—back to St. Charles Avenue, where they finally stopped to catch their breath. Chloe's short brown hair was standing up more spiky than usual. Her red-framed glasses had been knocked askew on her nose.

"Your shoe. We have to go back," Sam said.

"Not now. I'll get it later. I'll walk into the house barefoot. Mom won't notice anything. I'll put on other shoes. It's OK. Let's go. We have something else to do."

"What are you talking about? It's late."

"Right," Chloe said, "but we need to do two things. We should check out your garage to see if it's OK for the puppy. Then we need to go to Truman's house."

"You're crazy. I'm not going anywhere near that guy's house."

"Even to let the air out of the tires on his precious new bike? Come on, Sam. You've gotta fight back," she taunted him.

"Chloe."

"Come on. We can mess up his science project, too. He left it on the front porch. I saw it on the way to your house. He'll get in big trouble, and he deserves every bit of it."

"Chloe."

"Come on."

Sam knew there was little point in arguing. They headed toward Sam's garage. And after that, they walked toward Truman's house—a smaller, shabbier house than either Sam's or Chloe's and just one block over from Sam's.

CHAPTER 4

Anniversary

George Walton hadn't been able to get out of bed this morning. He kept trying, but also kept pulling the covers up over his head and dissolving back into a fitful sleep.

"Why can't I get up today?" he wondered, as he dozed off yet again.

"George?" It was Kay, his wife, with coffee. "It's late. You need to get moving."

"I don't know what's wrong with me. I feel like I'm trying to wade through Jello. Maybe the coffee will help."

George pushed himself up, swung his legs around, and sat on the side of the bed. He drank the coffee and still felt awful.

Kay walked over to the closet, reached inside to grab a blouse, and in the process glanced at the calendar on the wall. Then she understood what was wrong with her husband.

"Oh, George. We forgot."

"What? What'd we forget?"

"Today. The anniversary. Sam."

"Oh, God, no wonder I feel terrible. I need espresso if I'm going to get through today. Would you fire up the espresso machine while I take a quick shower?"

As she walked into the kitchen of their Athens, Georgia, home, she thought how much she hated this day. Every year, she dreaded it—the anniversary of the day George's best friend, Sam McCormick, had been shot and killed in Iraq. The memory rendered George useless every single year at this time. He could barely think. Couldn't make decisions. Sometimes he felt he could hardly walk across the floor.

Everything changed six years ago on this day. Kay's husband went from the always happy-go-lucky man she married to a man who sometimes had to work just to produce a smile, a man who, some days, couldn't seem to find the joy in life. Most days he managed fairly well—even though he was a different man from the one he was before Big Sam was killed—but not today. Today would be an emotional chore for him, from beginning to end.

Kay had come to believe that if she could get George back to the Atlanta Dragway, back into the drag racing world, it might help, but he hadn't gone near that strip nor any other drag strip since he was first hit with the news that Big Sam had died in Iraq—right when they'd had such big plans.

Once again, Kay silently vowed to work on this.

Looking around to be sure George wasn't coming her way, she opened the kitchen drawer where she had put the schedule for the current racing season.

Kay needed a plan. As she sipped her own cup of espresso, she sat with her reading glasses perched low on her nose and studied the schedule.

CHAPTER 5
Bicycle and Science Project

"Shhh. Now. Go now," Chloe said. They were squatting behind a bush in Truman's front yard.

"This is insane."

"You have to do it. It won't work if I do it."

"He'll kill me."

"Sam, go now! I can see them watching TV in the kitchen. It's the news. I can hear Brian Williams. Just do it."

Squeeeaaak. Sam opened the screen door leading to Truman's front porch. And there it was. The science project that was due tomorrow. Sam couldn't believe it. He didn't know what it was, but there were jars, and it looked like Truman had been growing things inside the jars. It was just too tempting. Suddenly Sam's fear gave way to, well, something. Bravery? Idiocy? Complete stupidity? All of Sam's pent-up anger at Truman erupted, and Sam went a little crazy.

Crash. Bang.

"Yahoo."

Chloe stood up from her post behind a bush. What was she hearing? What was he doing? OMG! Sam was laughing hysterically and ripping Truman's science project to shreds. He was throwing parts of it through the open door into the living room. Glass jars were shattering.

"SAAAAAAAAAAAM," Chloe yelled. "Get out of there."

Truman tore through the living room, took a leap, knocked Sam flat on his belly. Truman was tall for his age; Sam short for his. Chloe figured Sam didn't stand a chance without her help. She sprang onto the porch and used her foot that still wore a shoe to kick Truman on the leg, causing him to flop over, just long enough for a panting Sam to scoot out of his clutches. Sam and Chloe took a running jump off the porch, missing the steps entirely. As they scrambled off through the yard, Truman was on their heels. Sam's face, for the second time that day, was nearly as red as his hair.

Just as they started to make a little headway, Chloe remembered.

"Stop. We have to stop," Chloe managed.

"Don't be crazy. Ruuunnnn."

"The pup. We forgot the pup."

Sam came to such an immediate stop that Chloe crashed into his back.

"Ouch. Get off of me."

"Back at ya."

And here came Truman around a curve. They could hear him.

Sam pulled Chloe down to the ground, wrapped his arms around her, and rolled both of them to rest under an SUV parked on the street.

They were breathing so hard they were sure Truman would hear them, but apparently he was breathing pretty hard himself. The tall, lanky, dark-haired Truman stood on the sidewalk next to them, bent over with his hands on his knees, catching his breath, saying swear words. He had lost them.

Sam and Chloe tried not to breathe for what seemed like half an hour.

Finally, Truman straightened up, looked around, shrugged his broad shoulders, then turned and headed for home.

Now, they had to get the pup. And also let the air out of Truman's bike tires.

"Let's go around back and wait until it gets darker. We can't let him see us. He'll kill us both," Chloe whispered as they crawled out from under the SUV.

"But the puppy. We can't let Truman see the pup. He'll torture it just to watch it suffer."

"There's no other way," Chloe declared. "Come on."

They walked around the far side of the McVey's house, which was next door to Truman's. Then they slowly crawled into Truman's yard and settled in behind the shed out back. And they waited.

CHAPTER 6
Grandmom

Claire's phone rang. She picked up the cordless, knowing it would be her mother, who always called on the sad anniversary. Her friends, on the other hand, mostly left her alone on this day, understanding that she preferred solitude.

She turned off the burners on the stove, sat down on the overstuffed cushion in the kitchen's window seat, and pushed her blond bangs back until they were standing on end. She checked the caller ID, saw that, indeed, it was her mom calling, and pressed the "talk" button on the handset.

"Hi, Mom."

"Sweetie, how are you doing? How is Sammy?"

"Mom, I'm OK, but I'm afraid Sammy isn't doing well. He gets picked on by the kids at school. He has only one friend, Chloe—Kathleen's daughter. Nothing much has changed on that front."

"How's his schoolwork?"

"Terrible. His teacher said he shows no interest in anything. He doesn't pay attention. He's barely squeaking by."

"I have an idea."

"I don't want to do anything drastic. Sammy just needs some interests. We'll work this out."

"Summer vacation."

"What about it?" Claire asked as she walked to the front of the house and gazed out, expecting to see Sammy coming home any minute. It was getting dark.

"Look. It's only a few months until school gets out for the summer. Let Sammy come here. You know he loves the farm. Maybe it will do him good to get away, help his pop."

"Oh, I don't know. I don't know what I would do without him."

"And what will you do with him if he can't be happy?"

"You mean just leave him there with you for the whole summer?"

"Well, it's not like it would be a prison sentence, you know. We are his grandparents."

"Mmmm," Claire said, returning to the kitchen and walking out onto the deck, thinking Sammy might come in the back way.

"I want you to think about this. Maybe Sammy needs a change of scenery. You know, fresh air. Country life. Ye-haw!"

"You're talking about weeks! Maybe if we started with just one week."

"That's not long enough, and you know it. I'm not going to hurt him for god sakes. He's my grandson. Look, just plan on it."

"Mom."

"Good!" the older woman declared. "Then it's planned. When's the last day of school? Oh, never mind, I'll find out. We'll be there the following day. Good night now. Don't go browsing in that old trunk. Big Sam is gone. He's gone to a happier place. Nothing you can do but remember the good. Focus on Sammy. He's the one."

"Right."

Click. Claire's mother's voice was gone. And, as always, Claire knew she was right, except about the trunk. But a summer without her son somehow didn't cheer her.

Claire turned on the outside lights, hoping Sammy would show up soon.

CHAPTER 7

Tire

Well, well, what do we have here? A little puppy dog. Come here, little doggie. Let's play a little game," Truman said as soon as he spotted the pooch.

Woof.

"Tru." Chloe slapped her hand over Sam's mouth before he had a chance to finish his thought.

"Shhh," she whispered.

"But." Slap. She covered Sam's mouth again.

It was late dusk, almost dark. They could barely see Truman, and they couldn't see the dog at all.

Then it yelped.

Sam sprang forward. Chloe pulled him back.

"Wait," she whispered.

Then the two of them stretched out on their bellies and began crawling ever so slowly toward Truman and the dog. They could just make out Truman's shape, standing under an oak tree in his backyard.

Yelp.

Chloe put her hand on Sam's, silently urging him to wait until they could figure things out. And she thought she saw their chance. Squinting, she saw Truman's bike parked near the driveway. If anything would get him to release the dog it would be the realization that his Schwinn Scorcher was in danger.

Yelp. Yelp.

It sounded like Truman was hurting the dog, but they couldn't see what exactly he was doing.

Chloe pointed to a pin on the lapel of her pink denim jacket. It was a miniature jeweled guitar. Her Uncle Phil, a musician, had given it to her for her birthday. It was so dark Sam could barely see it. He moved his head closer and squinted. Chloe removed the piece of jewelry from her jacket and opened the pin on the back, holding it out for Sam to see.

Realization dawned on him. He gave Chloe the thumbs up, then he pointed at the pin, them himself. Chloe nodded. She handed the pin to Sam, then held up three fingers in front of Sam's face. They had been in rough spots before. He knew what this meant: On three, action.

Chloe held up one finger. Both kids slowly rose up from their prone position.

She held up a second finger, and they moved as quietly as possible to their feet. Truman jerked his head around. He had heard.

"Three," Chloe screamed as she ran straight for the pup, which Truman was holding apparently too tightly around its middle. Just as Truman reached out to punch Chloe, Sam screamed.

"Flat tire!" he yelled at the top of his lungs just as he stabbed the back tire again and again with Chloe's pin.

Ssssssssssssss.

Truman heard it, and in his rage, he let go of the pup, which dashed into Chloe's arms.

Sam, Chloe, and the pup took off, leaving Truman in a heap, crouched beside his damaged bicycle.

"Ouch," Chloe said. "Ouch. Ouch." She was still shoeless on one foot. But she kept going.

CHAPTER 8
Police

"Sammy, where have you been?" asked Claire as her son finally came into the kitchen, well after dark.

"Uh," Sam said.

"I've been worried sick. You know not to stay out after dark. Oh, God, have you been fighting again? Your clothes are filthy. And what are these scratches on your face?"

"Nothing."

"Sammy."

"Mom, it's OK."

"OK. How was school today?"

"OK."

"Did you see Truman? Did you try to be nice to him?"

"He's a jerk."

"Sammy."

"Mom!"

Ringgggg.

"Sammy, get the phone, will you, while I start dinner again. Your grandmother interrupted me earlier."

Sam answered.

"It's for you," he said, putting down the receiver before disappearing up to his room.

Back down in the kitchen, Claire was getting an earful from Truman's stepfather. He told Claire he was going to call the police because Sam had punctured Truman's bike tire and wrecked his science project.

Claire hung up, put her head on the kitchen table, and began to cry. This was the last thing she needed on this day, of all days.

Sam, who had listened on the extension in his room, put the receiver in place, then pulled up both his arms and bounced the heels of his hands off his forehead. Sam couldn't believe this had happened. He looked up toward the heavens.

"Now what?" he asked himself. "The police! No way."

Sam sat on his bed and thought for several minutes. Next, he stood up, shook his head forward once, put his hands on his hips, and said, again to himself, "OK."

Then Sam crawled out a side window onto an awning. Reaching over the awning to the brace that held it in place, he swung himself down, dropped to the ground, and dashed off into the night.

CHAPTER 9

Escape

"C hloe, wake up," said Kathleen Mullin. She was standing in her daughter's darkened bedroom, wearing the Georgia Tech T-shirt she was sleeping in before the phone call woke her up at 11 p.m. "Sam has gone missing. Do you know where he is?"

"What are you saying? What time is it?"

"It's Sam. When was the last time you saw him?"

"This afternoon. Why?" Chloe asked, yawning. "I saw him just before I came home."

"Claire just called. Sam's been gone for hours. She's been all over the neighborhood. She's about to call the police. And so is Truman's dad."

Chloe was exhausted. She had just taken her turn at caring for the puppy in Sam's garage. She knew Sam had been there for his turn because there was fresh food and the water bowl was full. But she felt she couldn't tell her mom about any of this.

"I'm sure he's fine," was all she could say.

"Chloe?"

"Sam will be fine," she answered. "He can take care of himself."

"Don't let me find out you know something you're not telling," her mother said, then left Chloe's room.

Chloe sat up in bed, stretched, and turned on her bedside lamp. She reached down to pet her dachshund, Herman, who was snoozing at the foot of her bed, and realized she was staring directly at—Sam! His head was peeking out of her closet.

"What are you doing? You can't be here."

Grrrr, Herman reacted.

"Shhhhhhh. Herman," Sam said. "It's me." The old dog went back to sleep.

"Sam."

"Shhhh. I need help. I'm leaving."

"What are you talking about? You're not going anywhere. What's all this stuff about the police, Sam? I can't believe you broke into my room. You should go home."

"I need some food. I'm going to my grandparents'."

"Yeah, right, you're going to walk all the way to Commerce?" Chloe had been with Sam to visit his grandparents many times. "I don't think so. Go home. Now."

"Chloe, I'm hungry. Can't we get your crazy uncle to help me, to help us?"

"Us?"

"Well, OK, me."

"You tell me what's going on. Then I'll think about it."

Sam told Chloe about listening on the extension when Truman's stepfather called his mom and threatened to call the police. Once again, Chloe realized Sam was going to get in trouble while Truman came out looking innocent. Not fair.

"OK, what do you want?"

"To go to my grandparents' farm."

"Tonight?"

"Yeah."

Chloe thought for what seemed, to Sam, an awfully long time. He was hungry. It'd been an energetic day, and it wasn't over yet.

"We'll have to take the puppy. Uncle Phil will help."

Chloe made Sam get out of her closet so she could change out of her pajamas, then she gave Herman a parting pat on the head and off they went.

CHAPTER 10

Garage

can't believe you did that. What were you thinking?" George Walton asked his wife. "I am not going to the drag strip. Call Kirby back, and tell him I won't be there Saturday or any other day."

Kay had taken it upon herself to call George's buddy Kirby to tell him George would be returning to the drag strip. She tried to tell George about it at dinner, but she couldn't get the words out. Hours had passed. It was late. So she finally let the cat out of the bag. And it wasn't going well.

"George, I thought it would help. No, I'm sure it will help."

"Help what? Help who exactly?"

"You."

"I don't need help."

"George, you do."

"What are you talking about? I'm fine. We have a house. I have a job. You have a job. What else is there?"

"Well, there is . . . happiness."

"I'm happy, dang it."

"Oh, I see. You sure sound happy."

"I need a drink."

"No."

"Huh?"

"A drink is not what you need, George. What you need is to get back out to that good old drag strip. Get reacquainted with your old friends. Rejoin the racing world before it races away."

"You know how I feel about that."

"Yeah, I know how you feel about that, and I am here to tell you that you are wrong."

"Oh, and since when do you know so much about what I need? I'll tell you what I need. I need a drink. Where's the bourbon?"

"George, just go. You don't have to race. It's just being with your friends. Goin' to the place you love so much. Just like it was when Big Sam was out there winning. There's a race this weekend. Please do this for me."

"Kay, you know it will kill me to go back there."

"I don't think so," she answered curtly. "In fact, I think that, often, you're already half dead, and furthermore I think you're afraid that going back to the drag strip will revive you."

"Revive me from what? You think I'm unconscious?"

"Yeah, well, you know you've not completely been yourself since Big Sam died. And you haven't been to the drag strip once since he died, either. Sam's gone, George. You can't change that. But you can get back into racing. It's the one thing you've loved as much as you love me and as much as you loved Big Sam. You've been partially under a cloud for six years. You can't deny that."

George poured himself a bourbon over the rocks and disappeared outside their home. They lived a short drive from the campus of the University of Georgia, where he and Kay both worked.

Kay peeked out the kitchen window and caught sight of her husband headed to the garage.

"Please," she called aloud to no one. "Let him pull that cover off his race car. Please."

CHAPTER 11

Car

George leaned against the workbench in his garage, sipped his bourbon. And he thought. He stared at the car-shaped thing that he could see only in silhouette because it was covered from fender to fender, tire to roof, in a shroud.

His mind raced back to 1991—the Johnson farm.

Big Sam had been smitten with Claire, though she hadn't yet noticed him or at least she acted as if she didn't notice him. And not noticing Big Sam was pretty hard to do. He was slightly over six feet tall, with broad shoulders, dark red hair, and intense green eyes that almost always seemed to be laughing. His easy charm was irresistible. But all the same, however cool she acted, Sam always found excuses to show up at her parents' farm. Did her dad need help with the cows? Could Sam help with the mowing? Could he clean the equipment? On and on it went.

Roy Johnson, Claire's dad, liked Sam and George. He gave them jobs to do and paid them for their work. And, in the bargain, Sam got to look at Claire while George got money, which was the main thing he needed.

One day, Mr. Johnson took them to an old barn out back, unlocked the door, and took the boys inside. There sat a car—but not just any car. There was something magical about it. Like a living creature. It sat quietly in the center of the barn. But it looked like a black panther that was ready to pounce. It was a 1966 Chevelle Super Sport, 396, 4 speed. Jet black with black interior, it looked menacing. Mr. Johnson opened the hood and nodded toward the engine: "This 396 cubic inch engine still makes over 400 horsepower—way more than an inexperienced driver could ever handle safely. This is definitely a car built to go really fast in a very short period of time."

Being seventeen and without wheels, the two were immediately enthralled. More than that, they were in love—love at first sight—with a car. They walked around it. They stroked the hood. They sat in the driver's seat, grasped the gearshift, and let their imaginations go crazy. Mr. Johnson smiled as he watched them.

That old Chevelle Super Sport was the beginning. Mr. Johnson virtually gave the car to them. The deal was that as long as they maintained it, they could drive it, and drive it they did. They polished and pampered their special chariot and worked on it constantly. And it wasn't long before they were itching to race it.

On Friday nights, they would drive the Chevelle to a deserted stretch of road up near Gillsville where they could watch a regular group of older boys race their cars while several more kids cheered from the sidelines.

George and Sam wanted to race, too, but the Chevelle wasn't theirs, and they didn't want Mr. Johnson to take it away. They discussed it over the next month or two, as they continued to be drawn to these illegal Friday night races.

Then, one Friday night, one of the regular drivers, Muley Evans, didn't show up. The racers needed another car.

"Hey, McCormick," yelled one of the boys. "Wanna race that black crate of yours?"

"Uh, no," Sam said.

"Chicken?" came the reply. "Buc. Buc."

"It's not my car," Sam countered.

"Buc, buc, buc, buc, buc," the boy clucked, as he tucked his hands under his armpits and flapped his elbows up and down.

"What do you think?" Sam asked George.

"Well, if we just do it once, Mr. Johnson will never know."

"He'll never know," Sam agreed.

"Well, chickens," the boy called out again. "Are you in it or not?"

"We're in," said George.

"Cool," Sam chimed in, as they headed for the Chevelle, got in, and moved it into starting position, up against a '70 Plymouth Road Runner.

It was hard to take the Road Runner seriously with its bright lime green paint and a horn that went "beep-beep" like the cartoon character. But this was one of the most powerful of all the Road Runners. The 426 cubic inch Hemi engine cranked out over 400 horsepower, just like the Chevelle. The deep sound of that Plymouth engine and the smug look in the eyes of the driver made the boys lots more nervous than they'd ever expected.

"Who's driving?"

They flipped a coin. Sam won.

"Hey Georgie," he whispered over his shoulder, "any idea how to do this?"

"Hold onto the wheel, give it the gas, and go fast as you can, I guess."

A skinny kid stood between the two cars, counted down, dropped his outstretched arm, and they were off—just seconds before the sheriff's car rounded the corner, siren wailing, blue lights flashing, brakes squealing.

"Yeah," George sighed and shook his head, thinking back on that night. He gave a little snort and then actually began smiling to himself. "That was the starting line. That's when the Christmas tree lights turned green."

Now, eighteen years later, here he was thinking once again about racing. He stared. He wondered.

Maybe Kay was right.

George walked over to this, his last and most favorite race car. He hadn't lifted the tarp since he parked it here six years ago, right after Big Sam's death in Iraq.

He put his hand on the roof and stood beside it. He walked around the car once, twice, three times. Feeling nearly overcome with emotion, he took several long, deep breaths.

Then, slowly, he peeled back the cover to reveal his beloved Pro Stock Chevy Camaro. It was always more than just a race car, more than steel tubing and carbon fiber body panels. It was a meticulous hand-built machine filled with special magic, designed to cover, from a standing start, a quarter mile in seven seconds at more than 200 miles per hour.

This was a race car that represented the best years of his life—all his passion for racing and pure love of the sport. The camaraderie of being with fellow racers, the thrill of managing a machine that was capable of hurting him badly if he made a mistake. And a machine that rewarded him with the ultimate feeling of accomplishment when he did everything right and won his races.

But more than anything, this race car reminded him of his bond of friendship with Big Sam. It always brought tears to his eyes just thinking about their days together—racing together—he in his Camaro up against Big Sam in his blue Trans Am. In George's heart right at that moment, he knew Big Sam would want him to go back to the single thing he, like Sam, loved so much.

"Yeah," he thought, "maybe it really is time to begin working on the car again, making it race ready."

George could feel his body trembling. A pair of tears raced down his cheeks. Next, he stepped back and let his eyes take in his first full glimpse of his great old racing beauty since that day the shroud went over it.

Then he approached the driver's door. His hand slightly trembled as he reached out for the handle and pulled open the door.

He reached inside and pulled the knob on the steering wheel collar so he could slide the steering wheel off. Then he contorted his body in order to climb in and get past the roll cage. Finally, he was cradled by the driver's seat.

He reattached the steering wheel and placed his hands on it, gripping it tightly. A chill ran down the backs of his arms. He gazed a long moment through the windshield and back into the past, thinking about all those quarter-mile races they called passes that he'd made in this very same car. He seemed to taste again the thrill of being at the drag strip, the general excitement he shared with Big Sam and his fellow racers. He heard the sounds, and he remembered the smells.

As he sat behind the wheel, he thought back on the whole ritual process of getting the car out of the trailer, tuning it, preparing it to make a pass. And he pictured all the fans roaming the pits, some of them asking for autographs, others just wanting to "talk racing."

George's right hand reached out to the first of the Hurst Lightning Rod shifters as his left gripped the steering wheel. He wedged his left elbow into the roll cage, just as he had done so many hundreds of times before. Then he clenched his eyes, took a deep breath, and pictured himself in the staging lanes, pacing nervously waiting for the final call for the Pro Stock class.

There's the call. It's time to fire the engine and move the car forward into the water to complete the burnout. George engages the line lock and hits the gas to spin the rear wheels and make their tires hot and sticky in a cloud of smoke. He glances over to see the other driver finish his burnout, too.

Now he releases the line lock and inches his Camaro forward to light those amber prestage bulbs on the Christmas tree. The other driver, whose face he can't see—maybe it's Big Sam—lights his prestage bulbs and moves forward to become fully staged.

George sees himself creeping forward to fully stage. His gas pedal is pressed to the floor—with the clutch pedal pushed down all the way—and he hears the engine misfiring because of the rev limiter holding it back to 8,000 rpms. The car is shaking, and the engine roar is deafening.

All the interior panels are rattling. His heart is pounding, adrenaline pulsing through his body. His eyes are fixed on the Christmas tree. Within a half second, which seems like an eternity, the amber lights flash down to green, and he releases the clutch.

As the car leaps forward in first, his body is slammed back hard into his seat by the force of a fast takeoff. Now the shift light flashes, and he pulls the shifter back to second gear. A second later he pulls the next lever into third. The world outside zooms by as he rips through time and space and now pulls the final lever into fourth gear. The exhaust emits a brutal howl as the big engine explodes toward its 1,300 horsepower peak in a ferocious rush.

George sees the finish line closing fast and instinctively looks over to see that he is ahead of the other driver. As he charges over the line, he lifts his foot off the accelerator, pushes in the clutch, pulls the parachute release, hears the reassuring WUMPH and feels the tug as the chute opens and begins to slow him back down. With this, the very best of all things has happened once again. In barely more than seven seconds he has hit 200 miles per hour in a quarter mile.

"Oh, God," he said, to himself and to his Camaro—and to the ever-present ghost of his buddy Big Sam—"Oh, God."

CHAPTER 12
Uncle

Get off of me," Chloe shouted, as she gave Sam a shove. He had fallen on top of her, following her out of the same bedroom window he had crawled through a little earlier. Fortunately the Mullin house was one story, and Chloe's window faced grass, not concrete. It was located on the side of the Craftsman-style house and close to the ground. So, there was really no damage done by the fall.

"Get over yourself. Where are we going?"

"Where else? Blind Willie's," she said.

"They won't let kids in there. It's a grown people's blues joint with a liquor bar."

"We'll go to the back door," said Chloe. "The manager knows me. I'll just tell him it's an emergency, and he'll get Uncle Phil for me. Let's go."

Sam and Chloe walked up St. Charles to North Highland, took a left, and went the few blocks down to Blind Willie's, the popular blues club where Phil, her uncle, often played. She saw him just yesterday, and he mentioned that he had a gig tonight. She knew her mother's brother would always help. Somehow he didn't seem like other adults.

Sam and Chloe stood in the alley behind Blind Willie's, knocking at the thick back door. But either the music was drowning them out or it was break time and the crowd was loud because nobody answered. Chloe finally pushed on the door, and it opened.

"Come on."

The two kids walked through the storage area and up into the bar section of the tiny Atlanta club. Uncle Phil was on stage, up in front. Tonight he had his guitar. Chloe recognized *Statesboro Blues*, a Blind Willie McTell song her uncle often sang. The manager saw them and told them they had to leave.

"Puuleeze," Chloe pleaded. "It's an emergency. You know Phil's my uncle, and Sam here is in real trouble."

"Oh, Chloe," the manager said. He knew her because she sometimes came in with Uncle Phil for sound checks.

"With the police," she added.

"OK, stand right here. Do not move. I'm going to get an adult to stand with you so that you are chaperoned. Phil will be finished in a little bit."

One of the waitresses found a spot just barely big enough for the three of them. Blind Willie's was packed. The waitress placed Chloe on her left, Sam on her right, and rested her arms across their shoulders.

Uncle Phil spotted them, and held up his thumb and index finger, indicating two more songs in the set. "He's cool," Chloe thought.

After Phil closed out the set with *Poncho and Lefty*, a Townes Van Zandt song, he sauntered over to Chloe and Sam. It seemed to take a long time for him to bend his tall, skinny frame down far enough to speak with the kids. Everyone told Phil he looked—and even sounded—like James Taylor.

"What's up kids? Past your bedtime, isn't it?"

"We found a dog. We have to go get it. Truman beat Sam up. Now the police are after Sam. We really need a ride," Chloe explained.

"Whoa," said Phil. "Let me get my things. We'll go down to Caribou Coffee and straighten this out. I can't deal with emergencies without sufficient caffeine. I take it your parents don't know you're here."

"No. Police," Sam managed to sputter, as they walked to the parking lot out back and found Phil's car.

"We can work it out, we can work it out." Phil sang to the tune of the Beatles song as he unlocked his VW Beetle.

CHAPTER 13
Wait

Mom, please come. I need someone with me tonight." Claire was distraught. Sammy hadn't come home. She called her parents, who lived in Commerce, about an hour up Interstate 85 North from Atlanta. Claire grew up in Commerce, on the farm where she first met Big Sam and George.

"I'm staying right here. I have a feeling Sammy is going to come here, to me and to your father."

"Mom, he's ten years old. He can't just show up at your place. How's he going to travel sixty miles?"

"He's my grandson. He'll figure out a way. And I hope he does. I'll hide him. He shouldn't get into trouble for retaliating against that bully boy Truman."

"Mom, you can't hide him. What if Truman's dad goes through with his threat to call the police?"

"If he does, then hopefully Sammy will be here, and I will keep him here."

"Well," said Claire, "he's not going to be there, and if you aren't coming here to sit with me you may as well go to bed."

"If I have to, I'll home-school him to see that he finishes his school work for the year. I've taught fourth graders before. I can do it again."

"Mom!"

"Claire, what is wrong with you? This is your son. Do you think Big Sam would turn Sammy over to the police? What'd he do? Mess up a bully kid's science project? Good for him. Ruin a bike tire? Who's to say that bike tire didn't already have a leak in it? I think it did."

"Um, Claire. Hello." It was a different voice.

"Dad, can't you do anything with her? I need you two here with me tonight while I wait for Sammy. Please come down to Atlanta."

"Claire, you know your mother. Do you think you should go ahead and call the police?"

"I don't know, Dad. Sammy's done this before, and what if I call the police and Truman's dad calls them, too? I don't know what to do except wait a while longer."

"Your mother thinks Sammy is coming up here. She's in the kitchen, already making soup and banana pudding for when he arrives."

"Dad, this is insane."

"And your point is . . . what exactly?"

"Uh, yeah. Look, Dad, I'll talk to you later. I'll call whenever Sammy shows up. I know he will, but I'm still worried sick."

"And we'll call you the minute he gets here, if you promise to keep it a secret."

"Dad!"

CHAPTER 14
Decision

Kay Walton stood at her kitchen sink with binoculars, watching her husband through two windows—out through the kitchen window and in through the garage window. She stood in the dark so that George couldn't possibly see her watching him.

She watched him as he put his drink down and walked over to the car.

"Please," she said. "Please."

She saw him walk slowly around the car.

"Go on," she urged, though no one could hear her.

She watched him put his hand on the roof. She took a deep breath.

"Just do it, George. Go on."

Then she watched him peel back the cover.

Kay put down the binoculars. "Yes," she sighed, "yes."

And she made a phone call.

"Kirby," she said. "What are you doing?"

"Kay? Is everything OK? It's late. Is George OK?"

George and Big Sam had met Kirby at the drag strip a couple years before Sam went to Iraq. And, since his death, Kirby and George had remained friends, but they no longer went to the drag strip. They went to football games together, fished together, even worked on cars together, but not race cars—not anymore.

"Oh, yes," she said. "Something has happened, and I think you need to get over here right now."

"Kay, is he all right?"

"Kirby, he's more than all right. He's over there in the garage. The cover is off the car. He's… wait, let me look. Yes, he's sitting in the driver's seat."

"Kay. How'd you do it? Hallellujah. I'm on my way. Might be a long night. Got any food?"

"I'm on it, Kirby. Breakfast will be served at 3 a.m."

"Can't wait."

CHAPTER 15
Sad Truth

Truman couldn't concentrate. His mom and his stepfather were drunk, their stereo cranked up to full volume—Hank Williams Jr. They were whooping and dancing—or, actually, stumbling—around in the living room.

He was trying to put his science project back together, in the dark. If his stepfather discovered what he was doing, he'd call him a sissy again. Probably slap him. Maybe beat him.

Truman was on his knees in his bedroom, with a flashlight, trying his best. He had worked hard on this project, and all along he thought he had a good chance for a real good grade. Truman's tears made it difficult to focus on what he was doing.

"I'm a country plowboy, not an urban cowboy," sang Hank, as laughter from the living room seeped back into Truman's tiny bedroom.

CHAPTER 16
Explanation

Double espresso for me, something sweet with chocolate for the kids. Make it decaf for them," Phil told the barista at Caribou Coffee.

As they sipped, Phil suggested that Chloe and Sam start at the beginning. So they did, first telling Phil about Truman's regular beatings of Sam.

"That's a real downer. Sorry to hear it, Sam," Phil said.

They explained about finding the pup at Callanwolde.

"Does your mom know about the pup?" Phil asked.

Sam said she didn't. Phil cocked his head and gave Sam a doubtful glance.

They told him about Sam going a little crazy and wrecking Truman's science project.

"It was scary," Chloe said. "Truman was furious."

"You really did that?" Phil asked Sam. "And you're here to tell about it? Pretty gutsy if you ask me."

Chloe pointed to her guitar pin, now back on her lapel, and described how Sam punctured the tire on Truman's new bike.

"It worked great," she said. "Thanks for the gift."

Phil gave out a low whistle. "I didn't know I was giving you a weapon for your birthday."

Chloe shrugged.

"Truman's dad called my mom. He said he was going to call the police," Sam continued.

"Sam sneaked into my room. We escaped out the window. And we came to get you," Chloe supplied.

"Aren't I the lucky one!" Phil said. "What do you expect me to do?"

"We really need a ride to Sam's grandparents' house," Chloe explained.

"And this would be where?"

"Commerce," Sam said.

"Commerce, Georgia? You want me to drive you sixty miles to Commerce? In the middle of the night? Without your parents knowing where you are? What? Do you think I'm crazy?"

"Well... " Chloe said with a little smile.

"I'm taking you home, right after I call your mom," Phil said, pulling his cell phone out of his pocket.

Chloe grabbed it. "No, Uncle Phil. Don't you see?"

"Yes, I see. You're going home. Sam will have to face the music."

Suddenly Sam was up and running out the door of the coffee shop. Phil and Chloe dashed after him.

He was part way up the block by the time they made it out the door. Phil got the car; Chloe pursued on foot. She was faster than Sam. She knew she could catch him. Besides, she was wearing her new hot pink Roxy sneakers.

As Phil pulled up alongside in the car, Chloe caught Sam's shirt. They both went down.

"Let me go, stupid. I'm not getting into trouble with the police. Let me go."

"Whoa," Phil said, separating the two. He had parked curbside.

"What's this all about, Sam?"

"I hate myself," Sam said. "I want to die. I'm not going home. If you take me home I'll kill myself. My dad had a gun. I know where it is."

"Oh, geez," Phil said, mostly to himself. "Chloe, I don't suppose you thought to... "

Before he could say another word, Chloe held out the keys to her mother's Honda.

"I knew your car wouldn't make it. I took Mom's keys. We'll leave your keys under the seat of your car so she can get to work in the morning."

"Man, she's sure not going to be happy with me," Phil said.

"Won't be the first time," Chloe tossed back. "Let's go switch cars."

"Oh, geez," said Phil.

CHAPTER 17
Diversion

Phil shut off his headlights before arriving at his sister's house. He pulled his VW Beetle up next to her Honda and stuck his keys under the driver's seat of his car. The three quietly got out of Phil's car, and Phil whispered that they should push the Honda out into the street before he tried to start it.

He slipped it into neutral. Chloe and Sam pushed while Phil steered. Fortunately, there was a slight downhill grade, so it was an easy job. Once the Honda was in the street, the kids hopped in, Phil started the engine, and off they went.

"Uncle Phil," Chloe said, "we have to get the pup."

"Oh geez," Phil said. "Sam, there's no way your mom is sleeping. She'll be up worrying about you. Where can I park so that you can get the dog then bring it back to the car?"

"Park around the corner on Ponce Place," Sam said, pointing. "There. Park there. I'll go get the dog. It'll only take a minute."

Actually, it took much longer. Sam sneaked through the backyards of three neighbors, but stopped short of entering his own yard. All the lights were on both inside and outside. And his mom was sitting in the kitchen, right by the back door. She would see everything. Now what?

Sam couldn't figure out how to get the pup, so he went back to the car and explained the situation to Uncle Phil and Chloe, who came up with an idea.

"We'll create a diversion," she said.

"Chloe, what are you talking about? Do you even know what a diversion is?" Uncle Phil asked.

"Sure. I learned it on *Jeopardy.*"

"OK, what's your idea?"

"The neighbors have dogs. They go crazy when they get out of their pen. If we let them out, they'll go straight to Sam's house because of the lights being on and because they always do anyway. They'll bark and run around in circles.

We'll have to be fast, but it will give us time to get in and out of the garage with Sam's dog."

After a very long pause, Uncle Phil finally took charge, just like Chloe knew he eventually would, being a big kid himself sometimes.

"OK, kids," Phil said. "Listen up. Here's the plan."

"Yesss!" Chloe said, relieved that an adult, or mostly an adult, was finally in control.

"Sam, after you get out of this car, go quietly and get as close to your garage as you can without being seen."

"OK."

"But don't move in to get your pup until you hear the other dogs."

"How do I keep them from following me?"

"Well, you might just have to run fast."

"Nice."

"Chloe, you'll let the neighbor dogs out, which will provide the cover Sam needs to get into his garage, grab the pup, and hopefully get back here."

"Got it."

"I'll stay here with the car running. We'll have to time this by counting the seconds. You two go in together. Chloe, you stop by the dog pen. Sam, how long will it take you to get in position after that, from the neighbor's dog pen to your garage? How many seconds?"

"Uh." Sam thought about it. "Twenty-five."

"OK, when Sam leaves you, Chloe, you both start counting to twenty-five. One Mississippi. Two Mississippi. On twenty-five Mississippi, Chloe, you open up the pen then run back here to the car. Sam, once I have Chloe I'll back up to the alley so that you and the pup can go behind your garage. That way, there's less chance your mom will see you. Does everybody understand?"

"Yep," Sam said.

"Roger Wilco," said Chloe.

"OK then. Go on three. One. Two. Three."

Off they went.

Almost immediately, Sam stepped in a hole and fell.

"Get up," Chloe taunted.

"Shut up."

Chloe ran into a lawn mower.

"Pay attention, klutz."

"Shut up."

They made it to the dog pen. For the second time that day, Chloe silently held up one finger, two fingers. On the third finger, they both began to count to twenty-five. As Sam counted, he made his way slowly and quietly toward the garage in his yard. Chloe positioned herself to open the dog pen. The dogs were awake and alert, whining a little, but not barking yet. They knew something was up.

Sam could see his mom, sitting at the kitchen table, her hand wrapped around a coffee cup, a magazine on the table in front of her. She didn't really seem to be reading, though, since she was sitting with her forehead propped in her other hand.

"Twenty-three Mississippi. Twenty-four Mississippi. Twenty-five Mississippi."

Suddenly, the quiet was shattered by barking, running, yelping dogs. The big chocolate Lab, thankfully, ran right over to the back door of Sam's house and made quite a scene, running back and forth from one end of the deck to the other, yelping and jumping on the back door in between laps. Claire—accustomed to this—walked out onto the deck and did her best to calm the dog. This took all of her attention.

"Perfect," Sam whispered to himself. He slipped into the garage, scooped up his new pup, and scrambled toward the alley. Chloe was already on her way back to the car.

"Come on," Phil said to the dark inside of the Honda. "Come on kids."

He had left the doors open to save time.

First Chloe flew into the front seat, panting. "Where's Sam? Where's Sam?"

Phil backed up slowly, keeping the back door open for Sam.

He was in position for about two seconds before Sam and the pup bounced into the back seat. Once the door slammed, Phil hit the gas and was out of there.

"Hey," Phil said. "Fasten your seat belts. Let's go to Commerce."

Then he started to sing, this time it was Willie Nelson: "On the road again. Just can't wait to get on the road again."

The kids laughed. The pup licked Sam's face.

CHAPTER 18

Mechanics

Kirby pulled up in Kay and George Walton's driveway. He grabbed his huge red toolbox and headed to the garage.

"Hey, old man, need an extra set of hands?" Kirby asked.

"Coffee's fresh," George replied, not even slightly surprised to see Kirby, who reached into the cupboard above the coffee maker, grabbed a cup, poured, sipped.

"Ahhh. You always buy the good stuff."

Kirby perched on the arm of an old leather recliner and looked around. George had the best garage ever built. Besides the usual things one would find in any garage, George's had a sitting area, a flat-screen TV, a top-of-the-line stereo system, refrigerator packed with food, soft drinks, beer. There was also a cot for naps or late nights. He even had a jukebox completely stocked with 45s. The Walton house could burn down and George wouldn't miss it.

Kirby put a nickel in the 1956 Seeburg jukebox. One of the eighty records moved into place. The Beatles: *Strawberry Fields Forever*.

"You're going to have to buy a new car," Kirby said. "This one will need too much work."

"I can fix it up. It deserves to be fixed up. Then we'll see," George said. He had removed the hood and taken a critical look at the engine before Kirby's arrival.

"Where do we begin?" Kirby asked.

"Brake cylinders," George said, moving to his shop, which looked a lot like a NAPA Auto Parts store, only neater and cleaner.

"And after that?"

"You know the drill. Start wherever you want. I'll take the brakes for starters."

"Nothing is real, and nothing to get hung about. Strawberry fields forever," the Beatles sang. Kirby hummed along.

CHAPTER 19
Sheriff

Turn on the outside lights," Essie Johnson instructed Roy, her husband. Sammy called him "Pop." Their eighty-acre farm just outside Commerce was perched a fair piece off the main road. And they were far enough out in the country that it grew very dark after the sun went down. Ambient light from the city didn't mar their starry sky.

Claire's dad didn't argue. He knew that Essie was expecting their ten-year-old grandson somehow to show up at the farm—an hour from his home in Atlanta—in the middle of the night.

And Roy knew that, absurd as it seemed, she was probably right.

So he turned on the lights.

"All of them," Essie said. "The barn lights, the lights out by the road. We want them to be able to find us in the dark."

"Who exactly is *them*?" Roy asked.

"Oh, I don't know, but Sammy is on his way here. I feel it."

"What's cooking?" Roy asked, mostly to change the subject.

"Chicken noodle soup, of course. Sammy's favorite. And I've just finished a banana pudding."

"What time are they arriving?" Roy asked, chiding his wife, but with a smile.

"In God's good time," Essie said, as the phone rang.

"Hello."

"Essie, you OK?" said a voice nearly as familiar to her as her husband's.

It was Billy Humphries, Essie's oldest friend. They had been in diapers together; their mothers had always been the best of friends. Billy was the sheriff of Jackson County.

"Billy," Essie manufactured a yawn. "Why are you waking me up in the middle of the night?"

Roy shook his head.

"Essie, stop it. I'm out at the road. I see all your lights on."

"Oh, that's Roy. He heard something outside. I'm in bed, Billy. Is this all you wanted? I'm going back to sleep now."

"Essie, are you telling me everything?"

"What's wrong with you? Have you finally tilted off your axis?"

"Essie, I have known you more'n sixty years. What is going on?"

"Not a thing, sheriff. Roy just got spooked. That's all. Now good night; I'm going back to sleep." She worked in another yawn for emphasis.

"Essie," Billy said, just as he heard the telephone click in his ear.

Then, to himself: "I know something's up. I just don't know what. Oh well, I'll drive back out here in the morning."

After the sheriff turned around and headed back into Commerce, Phil started the Honda. Chloe had spotted the patrol car as they approached the turnoff for the farm. Fearing he would be caught illegally transporting two ten year olds, Phil turned into a side road, killed the lights, and waited behind an old barn.

"OK," Phil said. "Sheriff's car is gone. Where to now?"

"Right up there where all the lights are," Sam said, pointing. "Let's go."

Phil hit the gas, and as the Honda pulled up in front of the Johnson house, Essie and Roy rushed to greet their visitors.

"Kids! Into the house!" Essie ordered. "Roy, take this young man to hide his car out back somewhere. Quick."

"Hello," Roy said, extending his hand to Phil. "Roy Johnson. Nice to make your acquaintance. Back up and head back over that way."

Phil said hi and followed Roy's directions.

Inside the house, Sam and Chloe were just about to dive into chicken noodle soup and grilled cheese sandwiches. Essie scrambled an egg for the family's new dog.

"You'll have to sleep in the barn," Essie told them.

"Cool," Chloe said.

CHAPTER 20
Missing Daughter

Kathleen Mullin reached over to her bedside table to turn off her buzzing alarm. She yawned, sleepwalked to the shower, took a quick one, then got partially dressed and headed to the kitchen. Kathleen stopped by her daughter's room and knocked.

"Chloe? Rise and shine!"

Kathleen padded into the kitchen of her small house. She put coffee on, plopped bacon into the skillet, set out cereal boxes. She poured juice and let two of the dogs out into the fenced-in backyard. She figured Herman was still in Chloe's room. She fed the dogs, turned on the faucet, filled the large water bowl.

"Wha…" Kathleen managed, as she glanced out at her driveway and saw— her brother's VW Beetle parked where her Honda ought to have been.

"Phil?" she wondered aloud. "Wha…?"

She went back inside, looked into the guestroom. There was nobody there. She walked back outside and looked around for her Honda. Kathleen scratched her full head of curly light brown—and at the moment wet—hair and came back inside.

"Chloe!" she yelled down the hall. "Time to get up."

She tended to the bacon, poured herself coffee, walked down to Chloe's room.

"Chloe."

Not a sound.

"What the? Chloe, wake up!"

Silence.

Kathleen knocked on her daughter's door before she pushed it open. No Chloe. The bed was empty, the window open.

"Chloe? Chloe?"

Kathleen dashed through the house in a panic, calling for her daughter. Kathleen thought she might faint, but she knew she had to act.

Her heart racing, she went back to the kitchen to pick up her cell phone and turn it on. She punched three, Claire's speed-dial number.

There was no ring. Instead, Kathleen heard Claire's voice.

"Hey, I wanted to call you first thing. Chloe is OK."

"What? She's at your house? Did Sam come home? Is my brother there, too?"

"Why did you ask about your brother? He's not here, but I know where he is."

"You know where Phil is, but he's not there? Why would he be at your house? No, wait. Why do you know where he is? Why is Chloe with you?"

"Kathleen, Chloe is not here, but she is fine. Come over and I'll tell you what I know. They're at Mom and Dad's."

"In Commerce?"

"Yes, Commerce. Hurry on over, and I'll explain."

"Sam's in Commerce, too? Oh, they are in big trouble. My brother, too. This is crazy."

"Kathleen, just come on over. We'll talk."

"On my way," Kathleen said. She turned off the bacon and the coffeepot, left the house, started walking, but looked down at herself. She was wearing her bathrobe. Her hair was wet. "Better take the VW Beetle," she thought, hoping her brother had the good sense to leave the keys.

"Ah, here they are," she said, feeling under the driver's seat and finding the keys. Somehow this comforted her. Kathleen drove the short distance to Claire's house, parked on the street, and headed up the stairs.

Claire had left the front door open. She was on the phone, but she motioned for Kathleen to come in and pointed to the coffeepot. Kathleen helped herself. Then she listened to Claire's half of the conversation.

"You don't know where they've gone?"

Pause. Kathleen could hear Essie Johnson's voice, but she couldn't make out what she was saying.

"Mom? Shouldn't you be looking for them?"

Pause.

"Let me speak to Dad."

"Mom."

Claire hung up.

"Please tell me what is going on," Kathleen said. "Chloe may be grounded until this time next year."

"Listen, the kids are with Mom and Dad."

"You already told me that. Is that where my Honda is? Phil stole my car and drove the kids to Commere in the middle of the night?"

"Something like that."

"Is he crazy? Why would he do that? How did they even hook up with him?" The two women drank far too much coffee too quickly as Claire explained as best she could.

"Sammy overheard my phone conversation with Truman's stepdad and apparently was afraid, so he took off."

"And, I am guessing," Kathleen said, "that he came to my house and got Chloe."

"That's what Mom said."

"So where does Phil come into the picture?"

"I don't know the whole story yet, but Mom said that Phil told her and Dad that Sammy scared him, talking about finding Big Sam's gun and killing himself."

"Oh, Claire," Kathleen said, her eyes filling with tears, "I didn't know it had gotten so bad for Sam."

"Neither did I," Claire said. "Honestly, as mad as I should be about the two of them running off and Phil helping them, I'm mostly thankful for what he did."

Kathleen opened her mouth to speak, but the doorbell rang.

A policeman.

"God help me," Claire gasped, as she headed for the door. "I think I am about to lie to an officer of the law." She opened the front door. Standing on her porch was the off-duty policeman the Virginia-Highland Civic Association hired to patrol the neighborhood.

"Good morning, Mrs. McCormick," he said. "Everything OK?"

"Um, sure. Fine."

"Sam OK?"

"Yep, he's fine. Couldn't be finer. Already off to school," she said, crossing her fingers behind her back because she had just told a lie.

"Mrs. McCormick, we received a complaint about Sam last night. No charges were filed, but a complaint from a Dwight Wilson."

"Oh, him. He's always upset about something. I wouldn't worry about it."

"You sure Sam is fine?"

"Yes. I'm sure. Thank you for checking though."

"OK, then, you have a nice day."

"You, too," Claire said, shutting the door and leaning against it, once again running her hands through her bangs, causing them to stand straight up.

Kathleen realized she needed to call in an excuse to school for Chloe's absence.

Kathleen and Claire had known each other since junior high school. They had been college roommates, and they had been in their share of trouble so they tried to cut their own kids some slack when they got out of line.

When Claire returned to the kitchen, the two old friends smiled then started laughing. Like mother, like son. Like mother, like daughter.

"We need to drive to Commerce," Claire said.

"Have you called in to say you won't be at work?" Kathleen asked.

"Yep, I left a message early this morning," Claire said. "You'd better call into your office, too, then we need to get on the road, hear this whole story."

"Yeah," Kathleen said. "I've got to borrow some clothes."

Claire called the police station to find out what she needed to do to file her own complaint about Truman. She knew she'd have to go down to the station to do it, but not now.

Kathleen pulled on some old jeans of Claire's, grabbed a shirt out of Claire's closet, and some shoes, too. Minutes later, they were rolling northeast on I-85, headed for Commerce.

CHAPTER 21

Walk

"Chloe, wake up."

"Huh? Mmph." Chloe turned over on her cot. Now her back was to Sam. She pulled the covers over her head.

"No, c'mon. Let's go," Sam said.

"Mmmm," Chloe sighed.

Chloe and Sam had slept on cots in the barn. Essie wanted them out of the house in case Sheriff Humphries came calling again.

"Chloe, I know the sheriff. He's one of Mimi's best friends. He'll be here this morning, looking for us."

She rolled over, yawned. "No he won't," she whispered. "We're not in Atlanta. Go back to bed."

But Sam was wide awake.

"He comes here in the mornings all the time for coffee. We're skipping school. He's the sheriff; he'll have to do something about that. C'mon, let's get out and go for a walk."

"A walk?" said Chloe, in an exasperated tone. She was still in her cot. "No. What time is it?"

"Early. I don't know. Let's go."

Chloe pushed back her covers. She knew when she had lost.

Sam grabbed some snacks out of the old refrigerator his granddad kept in the barn. Juice packs, bottles of water. He crammed everything into a knapsack he found in one of the stalls.

The three set out—Chloe, Sam, and the pup. Since they had slept in their clothes, there was no need to change into anything.

"Where are we going?" Chloe asked, biting into an apple.

"I don't know. We just need to be gone for awhile," Sam said.

"Let's name the dog."

"OK. Any ideas?"

"I've been thinking. How about Banjo?"

"Huh?"

"Don't you get it?"

"No."

"Uncle Phil."

"Yeah, what about him?"

"He helped us escape."

"So?"

"Uncle Phil plays the banjo. I think he would like it, and we could never have done this without him."

"Oh, yeah, good idea. Banjo. OK. It's good. Let's try it."

Sam called the dog. "Heeere Banjo. Heeeere Banjo."

The dog ran straight back to them as if he'd always been a Banjo.

"He likes it," Chloe said, just before Banjo took off again, running at full speed.

"Hey, Banjo, wait," Sam said, falling into a run behind his just-named dog. Chloe followed.

They ran as far as they could, finally collapsing on the ground.

"Where are we?" Chloe asked.

"Don't know," Sam answered. He looked up when he heard Banjo barking.

"OK, boy, OK. We have to rest."

They rested until Banjo suddenly insisted they get up and follow him again. This happened three more times.

"What's that?" Chloe asked, cupping her ear with her hand. There were distant sounds that they couldn't quite identify.

"Beats me," Sam said. They could hear loud, clanging noises and the sound of machinery. Apparently, there was some kind of construction nearby.

Banjo looked back and yipped for them to keep following. They obeyed.

"What is THAT?" Sam asked. Up ahead, he saw a huge facility like a sports field or a stadium or something, with bleachers, a big building, and a giant parking lot. But what was it?

"I don't know," Chloe said. "It's big though."

They kept walking toward the place, whatever it was.

"Hey look," Chloe finally said, squinting. "There's a sign. AT-LAN-TA DRAG. Atlanta Dragway. What's that?"

"Don't know," Sam said, but he kept moving forward, Banjo at his side.

The gates were open, so the three walked across the vast parking lot. There were restrooms and concession stands. Sam walked around to a place where he could peer into a big space. In the middle where he expected to see, maybe, a football field he saw instead two parallel strips of pavement with bleachers on both sides. There was a tractor pulling a machine that seemed to be either cleaning or scraping the two lanes that looked like roads except they didn't really go anywhere.

"What is it?" Chloe asked again.

"Don't know," Sam said, but he couldn't take his eyes off it.

There were workmen who seemed to be cleaning the place up, moving things around, making repairs, like they were getting ready for something.

But what?

Sam started walking around the perimeter, taking in everything with a strange intensity.

"Sam," Chloe said, but he already seemed to be in another world.

"Hey kids," someone yelled.

Chloe waved to the man as Sam moved toward him.

"You two gonna be racing this weekend?" the man asked.

"Huh?" Sam said.

"Junior racers. Are you?"

"Uh, no, guess not," Sam said.

"Oh, OK, well if you were, you're too early. We're just getting some things ready for this weekend," he said before he walked off in the opposite direction.

Sam felt funny. He sat down at a picnic table in the parking lot in front of a concession stand.

"Sam? What's wrong?"

"Don't know," he said, but his heart was beating faster. He felt lightheaded. Was he getting sick? He didn't think so. But what was it?

"You look funny. You might be sick. Let's go."

"No, no."

"There's nothing going on here. We don't even know what it is."

"I want to go in there."

"It's not open," Chloe said, starting back toward the gate. "Let's go," she called back over her shoulder.

"No."

Chloe had seen Sam get stubborn before. She gave in. "OK, let's go find somebody."

Sam couldn't figure out what was wrong with him. He felt drawn to this place and, in some odd way, to whatever went on here. He didn't want to leave. They walked around until they found someone.

"Hey, mister, can we go in?" Sam asked.

"Why? Nothing's happening 'til tonight."

"We just want to see," Chloe said.

"Well, sure, I don't see why not. This way."

And just like that, Sam found himself standing for the first time in his life on a drag strip. He looked up at the bleachers, at the big building at one end, at the signs, out into the parking area, and he felt… well, he couldn't have explained the feeling, but whatever it was, it seemed that he was in a place where he belonged. He didn't understand the parallel lanes between the bleachers, but he felt a little chill when he looked at them. He imagined the stands filled with people. He closed his eyes and thought that it would be exciting to be here when this place was open for business.

He had no clear idea what went on here, but one thing he did know for sure. He wished he didn't have to leave. Sam somehow felt that he loved it here. It seemed like some kind of home to him.

"Atlanta Dragway," he said to himself. He liked the sound of it so much that he tried it out again. "Atlanta Dragway."

CHAPTER 22

Transformation

Sam and Chloe were lost, but Banjo remembered the way home. The pup led; the kids followed. After walking for a very long time, they finally realized they were close to the farm. Without discussing it, they slowed down and surveyed the scene to see if the sheriff's car was anywhere around.

What they saw might have been worse: Sam's mom's car.

"Uh-oh," they both said.

But Sam was too happy, too stirred up inside—he wasn't sure why—to worry very much about his mom today.

They went in through the kitchen door and found Sam's grandparents, along with his mom, Chloe's mom, and Uncle Phil all sitting around the table drinking coffee.

Claire opened her mouth to scold her son then closed it just as quickly. She saw that Sam looked different somehow. He looked, well, what was it? That distracted tentative look that was usually on his face was gone. Sam typically held back a little, but not right now. At this moment, Sam was smiling. And when he walked through the door, it was with a confidence not usually there. Claire realized, good heavens, that her son actually looked happy.

Essie noticed something about him, too, and with raised eyebrows she signaled for her daughter to let her handle it.

As it turned out, nobody had to handle anything.

"Guess the great thing we found?" Sam said in a rush and didn't wait for a reply. "Some kind of a racing place or something. The Atlanta Dragway. It's so cool. There's something there this weekend. I think it's for kids. Can I go? I want to go. Will you take me, Pop?"

All eyes turned to Claire, who had gone white. Nobody spoke. Essie, Roy, and Kathleen were practically holding their breath. Suddenly, the three of them began shifting in their seats and looking a little worried.

"What's wrong?" asked Chloe. "Did somebody die?"

Roy Johnson regained his composure first. "How on earth did you find the Dragway, Sammy?" he asked.

Sam and Chloe both began talking at the same time.

"Sam woke me up," Chloe said.

"The sheriff," Sam added.

"We named our pup 'Banjo,' " Chloe said.

Woof, Banjo supplied.

Essie had filled her daughter in on news of the new pup in the family, so nobody stopped to ask where the dog had come from.

"Banjo kept running. We chased him," Sam said.

"Then, we found this race place. Banjo found it," Chloe said. "It's huge. We didn't know what it was."

"It's awesome," Sam said. "Can I go Saturday? Please, Mom. Mom?"

Claire hadn't spoken a word. She nervously got up from the table and headed outside. Her mother followed.

"Where's she going? What's wrong?" Sam asked.

"Chloe, let's go for a walk," Kathleen said.

Uncle Phil didn't know what was going on, but he knew enough to follow his sister and his niece.

That left Roy and his grandson in the kitchen.

"What'd I do, Pop?" Sam asked.

"Something that should have happened a long time ago, Sammy," Roy said. "Come with me. I want to show you something."

Roy and Sam walked out of the house and down toward the old barn, the one that had been locked as long as Sam could remember. He'd never been inside.

After a long walk, they arrived. Roy turned the numbers on the combination lock, pulled down, and the lock opened. He removed it, put it in his pocket, and swung open both barn doors. And there, having been backed in so that it was facing Roy and Sam, was an old car—a jet black 1966 Chevelle Super Sport.

Sam didn't know what to say.

"Come on in, Sammy," Roy said. "There's a lot of your history tied up in this old car."

CHAPTER 23
History

Roy sighed and poured out everything to his grandson about Big Sam and George. He told Sam about turning the Chevelle over to the boys. About the night the two of them raced for the first time—until the sheriff arrived and they got arrested.

Then Roy told Sam how the whole drag racing world opened up to them.

"Luckily, they didn't get hurt that night. Good thing the sheriff showed up or they might have been. No helmets. No safety gear. They had no idea what they were doing."

"Were you mad at them?" Sam asked.

"Me? No, not mad. Happy, really, that they got caught before something bad happened. They spent the night in jail."

"Did you take the car away from them?"

"No, I didn't, Sammy."

"What happened?"

"Well, son, I taught 'em to race. That's what happened. And they were never the same two boys again."

"You did?" Sam couldn't believe what he was hearing. "Like, what do you mean?"

"Sammy, your dad went on to become a professional drag racer. He was one of the best."

"He was? How… How come… Why don't I know this?"

"We'll get to that," Roy said.

"My dad was a race car driver!" Sam repeated, mostly to himself.

"A long time ago," Roy said, "my best friend ran the drag strip."

"He did?"

"Yes, he did. And I used to race a little, too, so I knew something about it. So after their parents released them from being grounded and with their parents' permission, I took your dad and George over there and got them jobs."

"What kind?"

"Well, first they just helped around the drag strip—cleaning up, that sort of thing. Some days, during races, they worked the concession stand. But it didn't take them long to learn how to make themselves useful to the drivers."

"Like what?" Sam asked.

"Oh, they learned. They picked it up. They both had a knack for cars and engines. It came natural to them. All the crews had to do was explain once, and those boys knew exactly what to do. They began earning good money, too, working as mechanics."

"I thought you said they raced."

"Oh, yes, they raced. That came a little later."

"In this car?" Sam asked.

"At first, yes," Roy said, "although soon they needed a faster car. But that's getting ahead of the story."

"It is?" he asked, his eyes widening.

"Yes it is. Both Big Sam and George raced officially for the first time on the same night—against each other."

"Really?"

"Two of the drivers who were already entered came down with food poisoning. They had eaten together that afternoon at some greasy spoon up the road. No way they could race; they were sick as dogs, but their cars were ready. Their crews were ready. They had noticed Big Sam and George as they raced this Chevelle (Roy tapped the hood of the old car), unofficially—just the two of them messing around at the drag strip. Those guys could tell that your dad and George had what it took. So that night they asked them to drive."

"What happened?"

"Oh, they both ran good races that night. I think your dad won. They raced against each other a few more times, too. One particular night comes to mind, but more on that later. For now, let me ask you a question. Do you know what drag racing is?"

"No," Sam said.

"Let's go talk to your mom, then, if she agrees, we'll ride over to the Dragway. How does that sound?"

"Awesome," Sam said. "Awesome, Pop."

CHAPTER 24
Sheriff

Sheriff Humphries," Billy announced, answering the phone in his office in downtown Commerce.

"Sheriff, this is Officer Allen down here in Atlanta. You got a family up there name of Johnson? Roy Johnson?"

"Sure do. Why?"

"Can you go by their house for me?"

"I guess so. What for?"

Officer Allen, the one who worked off-duty in the McCormick's Atlanta neighborhood, explained about the complaint filed by Truman's stepfather. After he heard about it, he stopped by to chat with Claire, who claimed Sam was in school.

"Then, just to be on the safe side," he said, "I went by the school and found out that Sam wasn't there after all. Now Mrs. McCormick's gone, too. I remember that her parents live up in Commerce—I met them once at a neighborhood festival—so I thought you might know something."

"Uh-uh," Sheriff Humphries said, "I see." And he thought he did see. "I'll run out to the Johnson place and see if anything unusual is going on. I'll let you know."

As soon as Sheriff Humphries hung up, he punched in the Johnson's number. No answer.

He headed out to his patrol car.

"Oh Essie," he muttered to himself. "What are you up to? What in the world is going on?"

CHAPTER 25
Stepfather

Dwight, could you give me a ride to school? I need to carry my science project."

Truman hated asking anything of his stepfather, but his mom was still in bed and wouldn't be up for hours. She wasn't due at work until later in the afternoon, and since she and Dwight had gotten drunk again last night, he figured she was probably passed out.

"Truman, you sorry coward," Dwight snarled. "I can't believe you let that McCormick wimp kid mess up your bike and your science project. Serves you right to have to walk to school with your project. The thing looks like a joke anyway. Besides, I ain't passing out rides this mornin'—or any mornin'."

Truman looked in the refrigerator for something to eat. It was full of beer, mostly. He grabbed a four-day-old doughnut off the counter and took it back to his room.

Truman fought back tears as he maneuvered his backpack—which held part of his science project—onto his shoulders and picked up the rest of it, which he had spent much of the night putting back together as best he could. It was no longer perfect, but it might get him a "C." He paused at the front door and took a deep breath. Once he stepped outside his house, he abandoned his sadness, cocked his head, and walked with that special swagger of his that dared anybody to mess with him.

"Wait 'til I get my hands on that Sam McCormick today," Truman grumbled to himself. "Just wait."

CHAPTER 26

Close Call

"Claire," Roy Johnson said to his daughter. "I'd like to take Sammy to the drag strip. Will you let me do that?"

"Dad," she answered, shaking her head. "First of all, he's skipping school. Second, there's a complaint about him with the police in Atlanta. Third, do you think it's the right thing to do?"

"I've always thought it, Claire. You can't keep hiding his dad from him forever. It was clear as the daybreak that the boy was noticeably happy when he came home after finding the drag strip. It's in his blood. You know it. You need to face it. And you need to trust him."

"Claire," Essie chimed in from where she had been standing in the doorway to the den, listening to father and daughter. "Let me take care of school and the police if it comes to that. Let Sammy go with Pop. You knew this day would come."

"Should I talk to Sammy first?"

"No, not now," her dad said. "There will be time for that."

"Claire, I think you need to go home. Let us handle this for now," Essie said.

"Oh, Mom. Maybe you're right. I'll let you tell him about his dad and racing," Claire said. "And you can take him out to the drag strip. But you know I will never let Sammy race. Never!"

Claire had always had a sense of dread about Big Sam's racing, but after she saw the video of the 1986 Bob Glidden crash at the Southern Nationals, her nervous dread accelerated to a new level.

Glidden was a champion drag racer, but in this particular race, his parachute malfunctioned. It caused his car to flip over about a dozen times. Thanks to the roll cage in his car, he walked away unscathed, but Claire could never get the horrifying sight out of her mind.

Claire and her parents walked back into the kitchen, where the others had been waiting and wondering if Claire would relent.

"Let's go, Kathleen. I'm leaving Sammy here for now," Claire said.

"You go on ahead, Claire," Kathleen said. "I'll ride back with Phil and Chloe. Call you when I get home."

"OK," Claire said, as she walked out the door to head back to Atlanta. As she slipped out, Banjo slipped inside.

"I'm taking Sammy to the drag strip," Roy almost shouted. "I'll go get the truck; be right back." Banjo left again, following Roy.

In the kitchen, Uncle Phil, Kathleen, and Chloe said their good-byes to Essie, who was packing up some snacks for them. While the adults lingered, Chloe walked out the door, then quickly ducked right back inside.

"Come with me, Sam. We've gotta hide. It's the sheriff."

Chloe took off in one direction; Sam pulled her the opposite way.

"This way," he nodded. "Cellar."

"Good choice," Essie said quietly to Uncle Phil and Kathleen.

The children climbed out a window and belly crawled out toward the cellar. Sam lifted the door, motioned for Chloe to head on down.

"I'm not going down there. It's dark and there's spiders. Look!"

"Just go."

Sam gave Chloe a shove and followed her down the steps into the storm cellar, completely dark after he lowered the door.

"I hate this. Is there a flashlight?" Chloe whispered, just as Sam located the emergency kit that Pop kept down there. A beam of light jumped out as soon as he found the flashlight. He got matches out of a metal box and lit a lantern. Thanks to the air vents, it was safe to burn a lantern.

"That's better. A little," Chloe whispered, as she stomped a spider. "Yuck."

In the kitchen, Sheriff Humphries introduced himself to Phil and said hello to Essie and Kathleen.

"What brings you out here, Kathleen?"

"Oh, my brother and I had to run over to Athens early this morning. We just stopped by to say hello. Getting ready to head back to Atlanta," Kathleen said, watching Phil suppress a smile.

"Essie, your grandson, Sammy, isn't here, is he?" the sheriff asked.

"Why would you think that?"

"Well, because he's not in school."

"Now how would you know such a thing?" Essie asked. "Of course he's in school."

"Have you talked to Claire lately?"

"Of course I have," Essie said with relief in her voice, thinking that the sheriff obviously hadn't seen Claire leave.

"And she didn't say anything about Sammy? There was a complaint filed against him with the Atlanta PD."

"Oh that. That bully Truman beat him up again, and his stepfather took it out on Sammy. The police ought to be bothering that family, not mine."

"You sure you've got your story straight?"

"Billy, what's wrong with you?"

"Just doing my job. I'll take you at your word. Need to be going anyway. Is that generator of mine still down in your cellar? I'd like to have it back."

Essie choked on her coffee, but, smooth as anything, Roy—who had walked inside a few minutes earlier—told the sheriff he just remembered it was in the barn.

"No, I'm sure it's in the cellar," Sheriff Humphries said, walking out the door. "I'll get it. Only take a second."

No one inside the kitchen breathed. Roy walked out with the sheriff. They moved toward the cellar. Below, in the cellar, Sam and Chloe heard voices outside and blew out the lantern.

Sheriff Humphries opened the cellar door.

Sam and Chloe pushed back against the concrete wall, hoping to make themselves invisible. They held their breath to avoid making any sound at all. A spider crawled over Chloe's shoe. Luckily, she couldn't see it in the dark.

The sheriff walked down one step. Two steps. Three.

Sam and Chloe figured they were doomed.

Just then, the sheriff's shoulder speaker squawked. "Sheriff, we need you back at the office. Pronto. Got a situation here," said the speaker voice.

The sheriff climbed back up, dropped the door back into place. "Well, Roy, I guess the generator can wait. Better run."

"Good to see you, Billy," said Roy, who looked back over his shoulder and raised his eyebrows toward the kitchen window, where he was sure the others were watching.

As soon as the sheriff's car disappeared up the drive, there were high-fives all around the kitchen.

CHAPTER 27
Drag Strip

With everybody else gone, Sam and his grandfather headed over to the drag strip. Essie got busy on the phone, calling in favors from some old friends from her decades as a teacher. After a couple of hours, she reached a tentative agreement with school officials in Commerce to permit her to home-school her grandson in Commerce for the remainder of the school year if this Truman business didn't sort itself out.

Essie didn't lie, but she also thought that it was unnecessary to tell her old friends and colleagues everything. She hadn't yet figured out what to do about the police, so she decided not to worry about that for the time being.

As for Sam, he found himself for the second time that day at the Atlanta Dragway. He and Pop were standing on the drag strip. It was literally a strip of pavement, just like a road. There were two identical strips.

Sam noticed a narrow vertical structure mounted at the starting line between the lanes. There were light bulbs stacked on either side of the structure, which looked a little bit like a stoplight.

Roy noticed Sam's interest. "That's called the Christmas tree," he said, "because when the lights are on, they are different colors—amber, well, some would call it yellow, plus green and red."

"What do they all mean?" Sam asked.

"Those lights, on race day, they tell the driver when to take off or if he takes off too soon."

"How?"

"Well," said Roy, "those lights are set to come on at different times to tell the driver what to do. First, as the car moves forward, the small twin amber bulbs at the top light up. This means the driver is prestaged."

"Hmm," Sam said.

"After that, the driver moves the car forward ever so slowly to light the small twin amber bulbs sitting right under the first two. See them there?"

"Uh-huh," Sam said, his eyes fixed on the Christmas tree.

"When the car has done that, it is staged," Roy continued.

"Staged," Sam repeated under his breath.

"Next, the driver waits for the series of those three larger amber bulbs to light. See them there, right underneath the small ones at the top? First the top one lights up, then the middle one. The bottom one lights up last. When the last amber light is clearly visible the driver takes off. That's how it is for junior dragster races; it's a little different for the pros."

"What about the other two lights at the bottom?" Sam asked.

"Right after that last large amber bulb flashes—in less time than it takes to blink your eyes—that green bulb lights up," Roy said. "The trick is for the driver to time it just right. If the car moves forward before the green light flashes, that means he has left the starting line too soon."

"What happens then?" Sam asked, staring at the Christmas tree, trying to take it all in.

"Oh," Roy went on. "That is not good. Drivers are disqualified for that."

"How can you tell if the driver moves up too soon?" Sam asked.

"Because the red bulb—the one at the bottom—lights up. They call that red-lighting. You don't want to do that," Roy said.

"Hmm," Sam uttered, still feeling confused. "So there's only one car?"

"No, there are two cars. See, there are two lanes here. One car lines up over there on that right lane. The other one lines up here on this left lane."

Roy walked Sam over to the second paved strip. "See, the driver over here can see the Christmas tree, too. Both drivers watch it, so they both have a chance to take off at the same time. Or close to the same time. It all depends on their reaction time and what racers call their dial-in, which is their prediction of how quickly they'll finish the race."

Sam looked confused.

"Reaction time means how long it takes for them to take off after that last amber light goes on. If they're good, they'll shoot off the starting line exactly when the green light comes on," Roy said.

"Cool."

"And dial-in, like I said, is the driver's prediction of how many seconds it will take him to cross the finish line. The driver with the slower dial-in gets a little head start, meaning the Christmas tree on his side will activate slightly ahead of the Christmas tree for the driver with the quicker dial-in time. Let's walk down to the end, so you can get a feel for how long a race is."

Pop and Sam walked the one-eighth mile section of the lane used for junior dragster races, stopping next to some large rectangles that looked like small billboards of some sort. Right then, both were black. There was one big board beside the left-hand lane; another one beside the right-hand lane.

"What are those?"

"Well, Sammy, a drag race pits driver against driver, car against car. The car that crosses the finish line first wins the race. These boards light up on race day, with two sets of numbers. The top number tells how quickly the car in this lane made it to the finish line. Elapsed time, it's called."

"Elapsed time," Sam repeated, trying out the words.

"And the bottom number tells their miles per hour."

"What is it, the miles per hour?"

"Well, junior dragsters can go as fast as 85 miles per hour."

"Wow. Is that fast?"

"Plenty fast enough," Roy nodded.

"Let's walk back down here. I might be able to show you something."

They walked back down past the starting line, and Roy spoke to one of the drag strip managers, who handed him something. Next, Roy walked Sam over to a big trailer. The man had handed Roy a key, which Roy used to unlock a big door at the back of the trailer then he pulled the door up to reveal what was the neatest thing Sam had ever laid eyes on.

"What is it?" he asked.

"It's a car, Sammy, a junior dragster."

Sam didn't say anything. He was stunned by the sight of this little car.

"Do you understand what this is?" Roy asked.

Sam shook his head no.

"It's a race car for kids," Roy explained.

"You mean kids get to ride in these?"

"No, Sammy, they get to drive them."

"They do? Like teenagers?"

"Well, yes, but also kids just like you, even before they get their driver's license."

"You mean I could ride in one of these?"

"No, Sammy, I mean you could drive one of these. Well, you could, but really you can't."

"Huh?"

"Sammy, your mom won't let you race, but I could see today how much you loved the drag strip after you and Chloe discovered it this morning, so I thought you ought to see it again, with me."

By now, they'd walked up the ramp into the trailer. And Sam could not believe what he was looking at—a narrow, long, skinny vehicle, sitting low to the ground. It looked like something that flew in from outer space, all pointy and science fictiony.

Shaped like a narrow triangle, it started at the rear end with two big back tires, each eighteen inches tall. In front of and between those tires was the engine. It wasn't covered but out in the open. Right in front of the engine was the widest part of the triangle, where there was a small seat and a steering wheel in front of that. There was no door and no roof, so Sam figured the driver had to just climb in. In front of the seat, the triangle got narrower and narrower until it ended almost in a point. At that place—the very front end of the car—there were two more tires, almost as tall as the rear tires but thin, kind of like bicycle tires. The entire car was nearly sixteen-feet long and painted in bright gold colors that looked like flames.

"Pop," Sam said. "You mean I would be allowed to do this—but Mom won't let me?"

"That's what I mean. But maybe she would let you do something at the drag strip. Just not drive."

"But Pop, I want to drive."

"I know, Sammy, but your mom said no, and that's that."

"It's not fair," Sam said, as tears formed in his eyes. "It's not fair."

He stomped out of the trailer without a second glance back at the race car.

CHAPTER 28
Second Escape

Sheriff Humphries parked his patrol car on the same turnoff where Uncle Phil had parked the night before. He had a feeling Essie's grandson was at the farm, and he knew that he needed to know why. So he waited. A half hour later, he saw Roy's truck turning off the main road down toward the farm. And, ah-ha, who could that be that sitting beside Roy but young Sam McCormick!

"Gotcha," he said to himself as he started his engine.

Just as Roy and Sam pulled up in front of the house and got out of Roy's Toyota, the sheriff pulled up behind them with his blue light flashing. Essie was out the door in an instant.

"Billy, you can't do this. I will not let you."

"Now, Essie, I am an officer of the law, and you know it. Sammy is a truant. I'm taking him back to Atlanta. Simple as that."

"Billy, this is wrong. Why are you doing this? You know Sammy's a good boy. Leave it alone; this will blow over. I'll make things right with this other boy, Truman. Atlanta has no jurisdiction here."

"Essie, you know I can't do that."

"Yes, you can!"

The two old friends were a foot apart, face to face. Essie was shaking her finger at him. The sheriff's hands were on his hips.

"Essie, the Atlanta PD has asked for my help, and I am honor bound to assist."

"Billy, that's the silliest thing I've ever heard. You don't have to do anything but look the other way. And nobody has filed charges. Only a complaint."

While Essie and the sheriff argued, Banjo strutted quietly around the house, observed the situation, then approached Sam and tugged on his pants' leg. The two quietly walked away, toward the woods. Once in the woods, Sam took off running with Banjo right beside him.

"It's criminal what you're doing." Essie declared. "You should be the one locked up, Sheriff Billy. Kids need love; not police brutality."

"Police brutality? Essie, calm down. Nobody's going to hurt Sammy."

"That's right," Roy said. "Because he's gone."

"Huh?" asked the sheriff.

"What?" Essie asked.

"Do you see him?" Roy asked. "He must be gone. I don't know where."

"Dad-blast," said the sheriff.

"Hot dog," said Essie.

"Now what?" asked Roy.

"I'm going to Atlanta," Essie said.

"What for?" Roy asked.

"To talk to that Truman's parents."

"Essie!" said the sheriff.

"Hush, Billy. Don't you 'Essie' me. And, by the way, don't you have some real work to do? There's no boy here; you can see that. Now go on. I've got to call my daughter."

CHAPTER 29

Cheeseburger

A little more than ninety minutes later, Essie arrived in Atlanta at her daughter's house. Roy stayed back home to look for Sam.

"Mom, these people are not nice," Claire told her mom about Truman's parents. "You just can't go over there alone."

"Claire, I'm a schoolteacher. I know how to handle parents. I'm going to speak to them alone, but why don't you walk with me and show me where they live."

Mother and daughter strolled a block over to Truman's house. Essie sent her daughter back home. Reluctantly, Claire turned back.

Essie knocked on a tattered old screen door. The paint, what was left of it, was peeling and dirty white. The screen was poked out on three sides. Truman answered the door. But he didn't say a word. He just stood there, hands in his pockets, a smirk on his face.

"Hello, are you Truman?"

"Yeah."

"May I come in?"

"No."

"Would you come out here and talk to me?"

"Why?"

"I am Sammy McCormick's grandmother."

"Sammy," Truman laughed at the name Sam's family called him. "That little weasel. I'll knock his teeth out."

"Truman, please come sit outside with me."

"What do you want?"

"I would like to talk to you. This is important. Is your mom at home? Your dad?"

"Mom's at work, and I got no dad."

"When will your mom be home?"

"I don't know."

"You know, they have great desserts and the best cocoa in Atlanta up at Murphy's restaurant. Would you go there with me?"

There was no reply, but Essie distinctly heard Truman's stomach growl.

"They have great cheeseburgers, too, Truman. Could I buy you a cheeseburger?"

"OK," he said, walking out the door.

Truman and Essie didn't say much on the walk up to Murphy's. She figured he needed to eat first. She didn't know how right she was. The fact was, his last real meal had been two days ago when his mom brought leftovers from work. She'd taken the last two days off and hadn't cooked during that time, so there really was no food in the house, except for some crackers and rotting bananas.

At Murphy's, Truman ordered a cheeseburger with fries, then asked if he could have chili, too. Essie agreed. She let him eat, making as much small talk as she possibly could with a ten year old. Then she ordered cheesecake. Truman ate two pieces, and for the first time he settled back into his seat and seemed to relax a little bit as he sipped at his cocoa.

"Truman," Essie said, "why do you pick on Sammy?"

"No reason. Well, not at first. Now, though, he ruined my science project and my bike."

"Why do you think Sammy did that?"

"Don't know."

"Truman."

"Because I beat him up."

"How many times?"

"A bunch."

"Exactly. What would you have done if you were Sammy?"

"Egged his house or something."

"Precisely. Could we make a deal?"

"Like what?"

"I make Sammy pay for a new bike tire for you. I talk to your teacher about your science project, and you and Sammy work together on a brand new project. If I get your teacher to agree, you'll have to do it this weekend."

"With Sam? No way."

"Truman, do you really like to be in trouble all the time?"

"My stepfather hates me, and I hate him back."

"Truman, will you trust me?"

Truman shrugged.

"Is your mom someplace where I can call her?"

"She's a waitress."

"Where?"

"At the OK Café out by the Interstate."

"Will your stepfather be home tonight? Before your mom gets home?"

"Yeah."

"Will you come with me back to the McCormick's?"

"Uh."

"Please. It's nice there, and there's lots to eat."

"Oh well," he squinted his eyes and thought for a second. "OK."

CHAPTER 30
Intervention

Mom, what is this kid—of all kids—doing here?"

"Claire, calm down. He needs our help."

Essie had brought Truman back to the McCormick house, where he waited in the kitchen while Essie spoke with her daughter.

"Mom, this boy beats up my son!"

"Yes, and we're on the verge of the police being involved. We have to solve this ourselves, Claire."

"And just how do you propose to do that? I'm sending him home."

"He barely has a home."

"How do you know?"

"Just because I took a year off from teaching doesn't mean I've forgotten what I learned during thirty years in the classroom. I want to talk to his mom."

"Why? I hear she's a drunk."

"She may be, but she does work. She has a job. She may need our help, too."

"Mom, Sammy is the one I am concerned about. Not Truman or his mother. Why are you doing this?"

"Because it's the only way. Will you trust me?"

"Do I have a choice?"

"Do I hear consent?"

Claire knew when she had lost.

"Whatever you think, Mom. If you truly believe it will help Sammy."

"I do. Now, I'm going out to the OK Café. That's where Truman's mom works."

"You're leaving him here?"

"Claire, he's a ten-year-old boy. You have a ten-year-old boy. You'll figure something out."

With that, Essie was out the door. Twenty minutes later, she was in a booth at the OK Café, ordering decaf from Truman's mom.

"Are you Truman's mother?" Essie asked, looking at the nametag that said "Tammy Wilson." She was a pretty young woman, but she looked worn out.

"Uh, who wants to know?" Truman's mom asked in response.

"My name is Essie Johnson. I am Sammy McCormick's grandmother. I would like to speak with you. Do you have a break coming up?"

"You mean that kid who messed up Truman's bike and tore up his science project?"

"Yes, Mrs. Wilson. I think you know why Sammy did that. Truman beats him up, you know."

"What do you want?"

"I want to work this out. I want to help Truman."

"My kid don't need no help."

"Doesn't he? Please give me a few minutes of your time. For the sake of both boys. Truman seems like a nice boy."

"How do you know?"

"Mrs. Wilson, I took Truman out for a cheeseburger earlier today. The boy was starving. And he had bruises on his arms. Is someone hurting your boy?"

Tears suddenly forming in her eyes, Tammy Wilson asked, "Can you come back in an hour when I get a break?"

"I brought a book. Is it OK if I sit here and read?"

"Sure," Tammy said, and turned to go back to work, wiping her eyes with the back of her hand. "I'll get you a refill. Would you like a piece of pie?"

"Thank you. That would be nice. I think I saw pecan when I walked in."

"Coming right up."

CHAPTER 31

Ham Sandwich

Roy couldn't find his grandson. He'd been all through the woods, shouting and listening and looking. So he started his truck and headed back to the drag strip. The big gate was still locked up, though it would be open soon for tonight's races. Roy found a way in—a back gate that frequently stayed unlocked for deliveries.

Banjo gave Sam's location away when he ran up to Roy yapping, then back to Sam then back to Roy. Sam was curled up fast asleep on a bleacher seat.

"Sammy, wake up. Let's go home."

"Huh? Oh, hi Pop. Where am I?"

"You're at the drag strip, Sammy. We need to go home."

Sam started to get up quickly, as if to run again. "No, Pop. I'm not going to Atlanta with the sheriff."

Roy grabbed his grandson before he could take off. "Sammy, the sheriff's gone. It's just you and me. Your grandmother has gone to Atlanta. Let's go home, get some supper."

Sam shrugged his shoulders and left with Pop and Banjo.

Back at the farm, the phone was ringing as they walked into the kitchen. Essie explained to Roy that she was coming home and bringing Truman with her. Roy started to argue, but he knew it was best to let Essie have her way. She explained what she had learned about Truman.

"The child is unhappy. He has a horrible stepfather who abuses him," Essie told Roy. "We need to try and help him."

"How am I going to break this to Sammy?" Roy asked her.

"Oh, you'll figure it out," Essie said just before she hung up.

Roy made ham sandwiches and put out some chips. He poured milk for Sam, iced tea for himself. Over supper, they went over what Sam had learned earlier that day during Sam's second visit of his life to the drag strip:

About the Christmas tree—"The red light is bad news," Sam said.

The length of the lane—"Um, one-eighth mile," Sam said, and Roy nodded. Then Roy broke the news.

"Sammy, your grandmother is on her way home."

"Mmm."

"And she's bringing someone with her."

"My mom?"

"No."

"Chloe?"

"No."

"Who?"

"Truman."

"Not funny, Pop."

"I'm not joking, Sammy."

"Truman? Here? I thought you and Mimi loved me."

"We do. Don't you ever doubt it."

"Then why would you bring that punk Truman here? I hate him."

"It was your grandmother's idea."

"Stupid. I want to go home."

"Sammy, will you listen to me?"

"I want to go home."

"Please."

"What?"

"Sammy, Truman doesn't have a nice home like you do."

"So what?"

"Some days Truman doesn't even get enough to eat."

"I don't care."

"His mother has a drinking problem."

"Big deal."

"He has no father."

"Neither do I."

"But he has a stepfather."

"Lucky for him."

"No, Sammy, his stepfather beats him—a lot worse than Truman has ever beaten you."

"He does?"

"Yes, he does."

"Why's he coming here?"

"Because your grandmother wants to make sure the police stay out of this. She thinks the only way is for you and Truman to work this thing out between yourselves."

"How?"

"Well, you know your grandmother. She'll think of something. Will you try to be nice to Truman?"

Silence.

"Or at least not do something stupid like throw something at him when they get here?"

"Don't know. Maybe."

"Fair enough."

CHAPTER 32

Bargain

Back at the OK Café with Truman's mom, Essie discovered that Tammy actually hated her husband.

"I'm terrified of him," Tammy told Essie. "I'm afraid to leave, afraid he'll do something terrible."

"I'm sorry," Essie said.

"He drinks," Tammy said. "Too much. And he gets mad if I don't drink with him. I'm a terrible mother. I get drunk to try and forget how miserable I am."

"Not good," Essie said, lowering her head and widening her eyes.

"I love my son, but I am bad for him. I don't know what to do."

"Will you let me help?" Essie asked Tammy.

"How can you? And why would you?"

"For my grandson, mostly, but also for Truman. Every child has potential, but they need help. Truman needs help."

"Dwight will kill me."

"Tammy, I can't tell you what to do with your husband, but I think I can help Truman. Will you let me try?"

"What will you do?"

"I'll start by taking him home with me, just for the weekend. Sammy has to help him redo his science project. I'll call the school and see what can be worked out. And Sammy also has to pay Truman for the bike tire he ruined."

Tammy sighed and said softly, "You're so nice. It's been such a long time since anyone has cared."

"I think you're nice, too, Tammy. So, may I borrow your son for the weekend."

"OK, Mrs. Johnson. I trust you. I know Truman needs help, and I know I'm doing a lousy job of helping him on my own."

CHAPTER 33
Sorry!

"**S**am won't like this," Truman said to Essie as they drove from Atlanta back to Commerce.

"No, he won't. No more than you do, Truman."

"Where will I sleep?"

"Well, I'd better not put you and Sammy in the same room. How about the sofa in the den?"

"OK."

When Essie and Truman arrived at the farm, Roy walked out to greet them. Sam stayed in the kitchen.

As Essie, Roy, and Truman entered the kitchen, Sam remained in his chair, looking down.

Truman walked in, feeling awkward, not knowing what to do.

"Now, boys," Essie said, "I know how you feel about each other, and I don't blame you, but this is going to work out. I promise. Now, you'll both be needing to go to bed soon, but first Pop wants to play a game of Sorry! with you."

"I do? Uh, I mean, yes, that's right, yes," Pop said. "I'll be right back."

Sam and Truman said nothing. Neither boy moved.

"Who would like cocoa?" Essie asked.

Neither boy spoke.

"Sammy, cocoa?"

"OK."

"Truman?"

"OK."

Roy returned and set up the game.

"Sammy, pick your color."

Truman laughed and repeated, "Sammy," in a snarky way.

Sam got up and moved toward Truman, as if to push him. His grandfather intervened, giving Sam a gentle shove back down into his chair.

"Green, as usual?"

"OK."

"Truman, pick your color."

"Um, blue."

"OK, I'll be red," Roy said. "And I'll go first."

Play began, and Essie brought hot chocolate.

It wasn't the friendliest game of Sorry! ever played, but for the two ten year olds it was a start.

Before anyone was close to winning, the boys started to nod off. Essie suggested bedtime and finishing the game tomorrow. Nobody argued.

"Whew!" Essie said to Roy once the boys were asleep. "We got through that."

"Yeah, but what about tomorrow?"

"I have an idea," Essie said.

Chapter 34
Chevelle

As early as she dared on a Saturday morning, Essie called the principal of Sam's and Truman's school. She explained the situation and asked if Truman could possibly hand in another science project on Monday with no penalty.

"You've got Truman and Sam with you in Commerce?" the principal asked, to be sure she understood.

Essie nodded, then, realizing she was on the phone, said, "Yes, that's right."

"And you think you can get these two arch enemies to work together on a science project?"

"Heaven knows I'm not making any promises," Essie told the principal, "but I sure want to try, and I hope you will work with me to give them another chance. Both of them."

"I see where you are going with this," the principal said, "but it's up to their teacher. "Let me have your number, and I'll call you back after I discuss it with Mrs. Flink."

"Thank you so much," Essie said, feeling suddenly much better about the whole dismal affair. "You won't be sorry."

"I haven't promised anything," the principal said.

"I know, but thanks for making the effort."

The two hung up, and Essie—who always looked on the bright side—decided to move ahead with her idea.

"Roy," Essie said, when her husband came down for breakfast.

"I know," he nodded. "You have an idea. Let's hear it."

"What about the old Chevelle?"

"What about it?"

"Well, I was thinking that could be their science project."

"What are you talking about, Essie?"

"Isn't there something they could possibly fix on that old car?"

"What? And take the car to school to show the teacher?"

"No, we'll do it with photographs."

"Huh?"

"If you can think of one or two things that two ten year olds could fix on that old car—maybe put in a new battery or add oil. I don't know, but if you can think of something, then you could run down to Wal-Mart and buy one of those digital cameras—I've been wanting one anyway—and they can take pictures of their work, mount the pictures on a piece of poster board—you can pick that up, too—and explain what they did."

"Is that all?"

"Roy, this is important!"

"You know, I really do think it's a crackerjack idea, Essie. Let me get some breakfast, and I'll head off to Wal-Mart."

Both boys slept late, and they'd just gotten up when Roy returned.

"Boys, after you get some breakfast, come on out to the barn. The old barn. Sammy, you bring Truman. He doesn't know his way around here."

No response.

"Sammy, did you hear me?"

"Yes."

"Will you bring Truman to the barn?"

"OK."

"Truman, will you come with Sammy and promise not to lay a hand on him?"

"OK."

"Good, I'll see you in a few minutes."

After breakfast, Sam and Truman walked out to the barn together—sort of. Sam walked ten feet in front of Truman. Not a word was spoken. Both boys looked unhappy. Banjo trotted alongside with Sam. When they arrived at the barn, Roy had the doors already open and the hood up on the Chevelle.

"OK, kids," Roy said. "Welcome to Truman's science project."

The boys looked at each other, baffled.

"Truman, you were wrong about beating Sammy. There is nothing right about that, no matter what."

"Yeah!" Sam said.

Truman turned as if to slug him.

"Whoa," Roy said. "Stop it."

He gave them a minute to settle down.

"And, Sammy," Pop said. "You were wrong to wreck Truman's science project."

"But Pop."

Roy cut him off.

"So here's the plan. Mimi called your school this morning and got permission for the two of you to make a new science project and turn it in on Monday."

"But," both boys started.

Roy was having none of it.

"What we're going to do is fix up this old Chevelle," Roy said, noticing Truman, who was poking around under the Chevelle's hood.

"Truman," Roy said, "do you know something about cars?"

"Yeah."

"How?"

"My stepfather."

"What about him?"

"He's a mechanic."

"Your stepfather is a mechanic? Has he taught you how to fix cars?"

"No."

"But you learned?"

"Yeah."

"By watching?"

"Yeah."

"Great," Pop said. "That may make this task a lot easier."

"Can I take the battery out?" Truman asked.

"Be my guest," Roy said. "But first let me explain what we're going to do. We'll charge the battery and change the spark plugs then try to crank the engine."

The boys were wide-eyed.

"But before and during each step, you will take pictures so that you can print them out, then mount them on poster board, and explain them to your class on Monday."

"Got tools?" Truman asked.

"Right over here. First, though, pictures. Sammy, do you know how to operate a digital camera?"

"Yeah."

Roy handed the new camera to Sam. "Then take a picture of the car first before we do any work on it. Take several so we'll get a good one. Then take a picture of the battery before Truman takes it out. Oh, and the tools. Take a picture of the tools, too."

"OK."

The boys began working.

The first positive sign came when Truman needed help lifting out the old battery. He looked at Roy, who looked at Sam, who gave Truman a hand.

"Next job," Roy said, "is the spark plugs. Know where they are?"

"I do," Truman said.

"Show Sammy."

Truman pointed to the spark plugs.

"There are four on either side of the engine," Roy explained. "A spark plug is needed to cause combustion for each cylinder. See these long wires that go from the spark plugs to this, the distributor? We have to slip the wires off the ends of the spark plugs—like this—and then use a ratchet tool to remove the spark plugs. It's really simple once you know what to do."

Roy showed them how to remove the spark plugs and then told them how they would need to pour a little bit of oil into each cylinder after the plugs were out. The boys started removing the spark plugs. At every step, Sam snapped a picture.

Roy noticed Truman looking at the digital camera. "Do you know how to use a digital camera?"

"Uh, no."

"Sammy, would you teach Truman?"

No response

"Come on, Sammy."

"You just hold it like this," Sam sighed. "You push here—but not very hard—until that green light comes on. It tells you the picture isn't blurry. Then go ahead and push it all the way down."

"That's all?" Truman asked. "That's it?"

"Yeah."

"OK." Truman took the camera, looked through the viewfinder, and snapped his first digital picture.

"Boys, I have an idea," Roy said. "Now that you've got the spark plugs out, I'm going to try to turn the engine over by hand, with a breaker bar."

He held up a metal bar about twenty inches long with a rubber grip at one end. At the other end, a shorter bar was attached, forming an L shape. This extension had a socket at the end.

"I'll do it," Roy said, "because it will take quite a bit of strength, and I don't want you boys hurting yourselves."

Roy fit the socket onto a bolt at the front of the engine. Then he rotated the breaker bar. After a few tries, he managed to turn the engine over several times and was satisfied all the internal parts were working properly. At this point, he figured it would be OK to actually try to start the engine.

"Is it OK?" Sam asked.

"So far," Roy answered.

He had placed the battery on the charger while the boys were removing the spark plugs. Next he would instruct the boys on how to install the fully charged battery. But first, he grabbed a set of new spark plugs from the workbench. They'd been there for years, but the box had never been opened, so they ought to be fine. He showed the boys how to install the new plugs.

"Hold it like this, using your fingertips to hold the center of the shaft," Roy said, handing a spark plug to each boy.

"Like this?" Truman asked.

"That'll do," Roy said.

"Here, Sam, like this," Truman said, helping adjust the spark plug Sam held. They went to work.

Finally, the new spark plugs were in and the battery was fully charged. Roy helped them put the battery back into place then he connected the cables.

"Well boys, we should be just about ready to start the engine. Truman, I would like you to pour a tiny bit of gasoline directly into the carburetor. Right here, on top of the intake manifold. Just put a little into the opening at the back of the carburetor. And Sammy, you sit in the driver's seat. When I give you the thumbs up, just turn the key to engage the starter."

"Roger, Pop," Sam said, getting behind the wheel.

Truman poured a little gas in the carburetor, and then Roy gave Sam the sign. Sam turned the key, and after a few chugs the engine fired and rumbled to life. Sam jumped out of the driver's seat, and the two boys now couldn't help themselves. Without thinking and with big smiles, they gave each other a high-five. Then they high-fived Roy, too.

"Can we take it out for a drive now?" Sam asked.

"Please?" added Truman.

"There is a lot to do before we can actually drive the car," said Roy. "In fact, we can save the rest of the work for another time. I am wondering if you two would like to go over to the Atlanta Dragway for awhile and watch a little bit of the junior dragster races."

"Oh, yeah," both boys shouted at once.

"You're familiar with drag racing, Truman?" Roy asked.

"Just on TV," Truman said.

"Well then, let's plan on going to the drag strip after lunch."

"Cool," the boys both exclaimed at the same time then laughed at what they'd done.

Essie couldn't believe her eyes or her ears when she showed up with sandwiches and soft drinks. Banjo yapped and ran several times around the barn.

"Essie, we'll eat in a minute," said Roy. "First, these two mechanics need to wash their hands."

"I can sure see that," she said.

While the boys cleaned up at the outdoor faucet, she set up lunch on a hay bale.

As they ate, Truman and Sam excitedly told her about their morning's work and about their plan to go to the Atlanta Dragway as soon as they finished eating lunch.

"That's about the best thing I've heard in a long time," Essie said. "I'm proud of you two boys. You deserve a trip to the Dragway."

Both boys flashed big smiles.

CHAPTER 35
George's Return

Why George Walton, you old son of a gun," said a veteran racer, looking up from the engine he was tinkering with, "what are you doing here?"

"George, good to see you," came the greeting from another acquaintance.

"Hey, George, what's shakin'?" asked a mechanic, standing up from his crouched position next to a tire.

"George, where ya been?" asked yet another acquaintance George hadn't seen in quite a few years.

George was in the racer's pits of the Atlanta Dragway, which—at the moment—were filled with wanna-be racers, fans, and racers, busy with the vehicles they would race later. Most of the drivers were from Georgia, but there were a few from around the Southeast. The place was filled with old cars—a '69 Camaro, a '67 Dart, a '67 Chevelle, and motorcycles, in addition to the junior dragsters. The adult races would begin as soon as the junior dragsters finished.

Finally, much to George's relief, one of the Super Pro class drivers asked, "George, can you give me a hand?" As if George had been here at the drag strip only yesterday instead of six years ago.

At last, something he could do. George hated being noticed. He didn't want anyone to make a big deal out of the fact that he was back at the drag strip for the first time in a long time. Gratefully, he agreed to help at the same time that he noticed Kirby heading across the parking lot. George and Kirby got to work.

His head was bent over the engine of a '95 Mustang GT when somebody caught his eye. It was a red-headed kid. Even though George was sure it was nobody he knew, he did a double take anyway. Then he went back to work, looking up one more time to search for the kid, who had disappeared into the crowd. George shrugged his shoulders and went back to work.

Finally, the junior dragsters were in their staging area behind the big building at the starting end of the drag strip. Roy asked Sam and Truman if they'd like to go back to where the kids were lining up, to talk to the drivers and get a look at their cars. Just anyone wasn't allowed, but Roy had a few privileges.

Sam first spotted the car with the golden flames that Roy had shown him yesterday. Truman had his eye on a white car with red, purple, and blue lightning bolts painted on the sides.

"Wow," he said quietly.

"Know anything about these cars?" Roy asked Truman.

"Not really."

"Which one do you like?"

Truman pointed.

"Let's go talk to the driver," Roy said. Truman and Sam followed him through an open gate. The area behind the chain link fence was full of kids, their cars, and their parents. A few younger brothers and sisters milled around, too. Everyone was busy with last-minute adjustments.

The driver of the car that Truman liked turned out to be a girl. Truman was speechless, but since Sam's best friend was Chloe it didn't faze him.

"Nice car," Sam said.

"Thanks," she said.

"How fast does it go?"

"About 75."

Truman found courage: "Is it hard to drive?"

"No."

"How big's the engine?" he asked.

"Five," the girl answered.

Truman and Sam were quiet, then Sam asked the question they both were wondering, "Five what?"

"Horsepower," the girl answered. "Briggs & Stratton," she explained. Then her dad appeared, and she climbed into the driver's seat and donned her helmet.

"Good luck," Sam said.

Truman was practically stunned. He just couldn't quite believe where he was, what he was seeing.

"OK, boys," said Roy. "Let's move back around to the starting line."

Just before the first two cars moved into position, Truman and Sam watched as a man took the covers off the big back tires of the junior dragster that would race in the far lane. For the car that would race in the near lane, a man wiped off the back tires of the other dragster with his hands. Then both men guided the drivers into position.

Before Sam and Truman knew it, the amber bulbs at the top of the Christmas tree lit up.

Sam pointed it out so that Truman would notice. They watched as both cars crept forward. Then two more twin amber lights came on. Both cars stopped. Next, Truman saw one, two, three caution lights come on—one right after the other, climbing downward. After the third one lit up, a green light came on and simultaneously the cars charged down their lanes. The red light at the bottom stayed dark since both drivers had perfect reaction times; neither had jumped the gun.

"Cool," Truman said.

"Awesome," said Sam.

The boys didn't move from where they sat until every car had finished its pass. They barely breathed, in fact.

Sam and Truman wanted to stay and watch the big cars race, but Roy reminded them they had that science project to finish. Reluctantly, they followed Roy out toward the parking lot.

Before they made it to the gate, Roy heard his name. The voice was tentative, and there was something familiar about it, too.

"Roy," the voice said again. Roy looked around through the throngs of people. Then he saw the source of the voice.

"Oh, my God, George! Oh, my God," Roy's voice cracked.

The two men dodged people left and right as they walked swiftly toward each other. It was difficult to tell who was having the harder time controlling his emotions.

They embraced.

"George," was all Roy could manage.

"Roy, I…" George began, then stopped and stared.

Sam and Truman had followed Roy.

"Roy, oh no. This isn't…" Looking at Sam, George cleared his throat, tried to regain his composure.

Finally, Roy gathered a little composure of his own, though his voice was weak and wobbly.

"George, this is Sammy and Sammy's friend Truman."

"Sammy," is all George could manage. His eyes were full of tears. Finally, he began to sob. He knew now why that kid he noticed earlier had caught his attention.

"I'm sorry. I'm so sorry," he repeated over and over.

Roy was crying, too.

Sam and Truman stood there for several awkward moments, dumbstruck.

Finally, Roy explained: "Sammy, this is George Walton, your dad's best friend in the entire world."

"He is? Was? You are? You were?" Sam managed to say.

George squatted down so that he was eye-to-eye with Sam.

"Sammy, oh my gosh, Sammy. I don't know what to say. I owe you the biggest apology. It's so great to see you, son. I can't begin to explain how great it is."

Sam said nothing at first.

Then finally, "Why don't I know you?"

Thankfully, Roy intervened. "George, will you come back to the farm with us?"

"Roy, thank you. Looks like I don't have a choice, but I would be honored."

As the four of them walked into the parking lot, Sam asked Roy, "Pop, is he the one who raced with my dad?"

George answered. "Yes, Sammy, I am the one. We have a lot of catching up to do."

CHAPTER 36
Arrest

"Pop," Sam asked, as they walked through the parking lot. "Would it be OK if I rode with George? Uh, with Mr. Walton."

"Sure, Sammy, it's fine with me if George doesn't mind."

"Sammy, I can't think of anything I would like better. It's OK if you call me George. My car's over here. See you at the farm, Roy. And Truman."

Sam went silent once in George's car. He had so many questions, but he didn't know where to begin.

Thankfully, George took over, explaining as best he could how everything had changed for him when Big Sam died.

"Your dad and I were in first grade together, and after that it seemed like I couldn't remember a day without him in it. We did everything together. We fished. We played high school football. And we played on the same Little League team."

"Was my dad any good?"

"At baseball? You bet. He could hit the ball like Hank Aaron. He was our own Home Run King. And he wasn't bad on the football field, either."

"Really?"

"Yes, really. When we got older, we double dated. I'm not sure I remember having a date without your dad and his date—usually your mom—being there."

Sam listened intently.

"When I got the news that my best friend, your dad, had been killed, my life kind of stopped, too. On the very day I got the news, I rolled my race car into the garage and covered it up. I just couldn't face racing without Big Sam. It's hard to believe, but I only uncovered it for the first time a couple days ago."

"You have a race car?"

"I sure do. Would you like to see it sometime?"

"Yeah," Sam said. "I would. But how come I don't know you?"

"Because Sammy," George said. "I couldn't face you or your mother after Big Sam died. I was devastated, and you two reminded me too much of the friend I lost. I decided to stay away. That was wrong. I know that now, but that's what happened. I'm sure you don't understand, and there's no reason you should."

"You knew me?" Sam asked.

"Yes, I knew you. I was at the hospital when you were born. I was at every one of your four birthday parties until, you know, Big Sam died."

"Have you been mad at me and my mom?"

"Oh, no, nothing like that. Now that I've seen you, I'm mad at myself. I hope you will forgive me and let me be part of your life again."

Silence.

"Do you think you can do that, Sammy?"

"Mr. Walton?"

"Yeah?"

"My mom won't let me race."

"Do you want to?"

"I think so."

"What does your mom say?"

"I don't know. Pop told me she won't let me."

"What do you know about it?"

"About what?"

"Racing."

"Nothing."

"You mean your mom never told you about your dad? His racing? And Roy never told you?"

"No."

"Then why were you here today?"

"It was by accident."

"What do you mean?"

"I was in trouble. I got Chloe to help me come to Mimi and Pop's. We went for a walk—me and Chloe and Banjo. That's my dog. He, um Banjo, took us here. Then Pop showed me the Chevelle."

"Roy still has the Chevelle?" George asked.

"Uh-huh. After that he brought me here. I messed up Truman's science project. We have to do another one. We're doing the Chevelle."

"Hmmm," George said. He had trouble following what Sam was telling him, but he got the gist of it.

"When Pop brought me here, he told me my mom won't let me race."

By the time Sam was finished talking, they were pulling up at the farm—right behind a car with Truman's mom and stepfather inside.

"Oh, no," Sam said. "Truman's parents."

"Is that bad?" George asked.

He got his answer within seconds.

Dwight got out of Tammy's car and ran straight for Truman, who had arrived a minute earlier, with Roy. Dwight grabbed his stepson by the arm, threw him to the ground, and planted a punch right in his ribs.

With a growl, Banjo grabbed Dwight by the pants' leg and wouldn't let go.

Dwight hit Truman in the ribs again.

"Stop it, Dwight. Stop!" Tammy screamed.

Sam jumped on Dwight's back and started pounding him.

Finally, another set of hands and arms entered the fray. Sheriff Humphries had arrived just seconds behind everyone else. After a struggle, the sheriff slapped a handcuff on one of Dwight's wrists, then wrestled the other arm around and cuffed it, too.

Banjo let go when Sam slid down off Dwight's back.

Both Essie and Tammy ran to look after Truman.

Sam bent down to ask Truman if he was OK.

Truman wiped his dripping nose as Tammy cried.

The sheriff put his hand on top of Dwight's head, pushed him into the patrol car, and closed the door. He reported the arrest into his shoulder mike.

"Essie," Sheriff Humphries said, "looks like we have the real criminal here, and it's sure not Sammy. Except for skipping school, Sammy shouldn't be in any other trouble."

Sam helped Truman up.

"Uh, thanks," Truman said.

"OK," Sam said.

Just then, Essie noticed George for the first time. She broke into a run and didn't stop until her arms were around him. They hugged for a long time.

"What's this I hear about a science project?" George finally said.

"Out in the barn," Sam answered. He, Truman, and George headed out to the barn together, with Banjo trotting ahead of them.

"Mrs. Johnson," Tammy said. "How can I thank you?"

"Let's see," Essie said, gazing around. "It looks like we have a crowd for supper. Can you cook?"

"It's been awhile," said Tammy, "but I'm sure it'll come back to me."

"Well, then, let's get started. While we cook, you can tell me what you're going to do about that husband of yours."

"That's easy," Tammy said. "I'm divorcing him. I already called Legal Aid this morning and left a message that I want an appointment for next week."

"Good girl. Since the sheriff actually saw him beating Truman, I don't think you'll have to worry about him troubling you for awhile. In the meantime, we'll figure out how to keep you safe once he gets out of jail."

CHAPTER 37
Take Two

"**A**nd then, see, I poured the gas in the carburetor. That's here in this picture."

Truman was standing in front of his fourth grade class on Monday morning, explaining his science project. Sam was holding up the poster board. The two of them had everyone's undivided attention.

Their classmates couldn't believe the change in Truman or that Sam and Truman were actually standing in front of the class together and not fighting. Neither could the teacher.

"And then Sam turned the key," said Truman. "And the car started."

All eyes shifted from Truman to Sam and back.

Finally, Mrs. Flink asked if the children had questions.

One boy's arm shot up: "Where'd you get the car?" he asked.

"Uh, it belongs to Sam's grandpa," Truman said.

An avalanche of excited questions followed.

"What kind of car?"

"Chevelle," Sam answered.

"How'd you know what to do?"

"Pop—my grandpa—helped. Truman knows some stuff, too."

"Was it hard to get the spark plugs out?"

"No," Truman and Sam said in unison, then looked at each other and laughed.

After the bell rang for recess, the discussion continued on the playground. Sam and Truman had been transformed from class bully and class victim into superstars.

"We went to the Atlanta Dragway," Sam told his classmates.

"What's that?"

Truman explained, and Sam joined in. They described the drag strip, told about talking to the racers, painted a colorful verbal picture of what all the cars looked like.

"Are you going to be drag racers?" one boy asked.

"Uh, no," Sam said.

"Why not?" asked another.

"Just because," Sam said, looking down.

"We just like going there," Truman said, "but we don't want to race."

"Right," Chloe said under her breath. "Like heck you don't."

Back in the classroom after recess, the teacher instructed the children to write a descriptive paragraph, about anything.

"Just describe something you like," she said.

CHAPTER 38

Secrets Revealed

When Claire got home from work, Sam declared, "I'm going over to Chloe's."

"Not yet," Claire said.

"But Mom, Truman and Chloe are waiting for me."

"First, you need to finish your chores. You're still working off the money I lent you to pay for Truman's bike tire. Then I need to show you something. This may take awhile. Why don't you just call and tell them you'll be a little late."

Sam wasn't happy, but he called Chloe.

He took out the trash, swept the front porch, and blew off the front walk and steps. After he was finished, Claire took her son down to the basement and unlocked the secret room where the trunk stayed. She pulled out the brick, retrieved the velvet box, removed the key, and unlocked the trunk.

Sam watched her as she did all of this, not knowing what to think or say.

"I have some things to show you," she said as she lifted the lid on the old orange trunk, which was about to reveal its long-held secrets.

First, Claire took out the trophies. Sam didn't understand until he noticed first one, then another, then yet another brass plate engraved with his father's name.

"What are these?" he asked.

"Your dad won a lot of races, Sammy," Claire said. "He was a nationally ranked drag racer."

Sam's words got stuck behind a huge lump in his throat.

Claire took out a fire suit, handed it to Sam.

"What's this?" Sam squeaked out.

"It's the safety suit your dad wore when he raced."

The lump grew.

She handed her son his dad's helmet. He put it on. She handed him the shoes. He put them on, too, even though they were too big. Next, out came a shirt with printing on it that read: Sam McCormick. Pro Stock. Sam put that on, too, but he still couldn't speak. It was all a bit overwhelming for Sam. He felt happy and sad and confused all at the same time.

"Here," Claire said, as she handed her son a small plastic rectangle with a number on it. "You can hang this in your room if you like."

"What is it?" Sam whispered.

"Your dad's number."

"Huh?"

"Your dad raced Pro Stock cars. They all have numbers. That was his."

"Three One Eight Three." Sam read the number out loud. "Three One Eight Three. This number was on his car?"

Claire showed Sam a picture of his dad's car, a Pontiac Trans Am, No. 3183.

"Yes, the number was on his car. These cars are built from scratch. Your dad's was, essentially, a race car that was built by hand. The car I drive was built on an assembly line and took only a few hours to build," she explained. "But it takes many weeks to build a race car like this.

"The engine in my car produces about 180 horsepower. When your dad raced, his engine produced about 1,300 horsepower," Claire went on. "Racers think of their cars as works of art—beautiful in detail and function. And even I have to admit the safety features of these cars far exceed the cars we drive on a day-to-day basis. Truthfully, your father was much safer when he was driving his race car than we are when we leave the house in our regular car."

"Where is it?"

"I sold it. I sold the race car, engines, transmissions, spare parts, the truck, and trailer. Everything. We needed the money. But here is his racing license. At least I kept that."

"Can I have all this stuff?"

"Sure you can."

"Can I put it all in my room?"

"Yep."

"Now?"

"Anytime you want."

"What else is there?"

Claire pulled out a manilla envelope and told Sam it was full of newspaper and magazine clippings. "Take your time reading these, Sammy. They're all yours."

"Mom," he said. "Why didn't you ever tell me?"

"I'm sorry. I should have. You deserved to know this part of your father's life. But I was afraid—for you, and for me, too."

"Why can't I race like Dad?"

"Because it frightens me. I was always terrified your dad would have an accident at the drag strip. I've seen it happen. I just cannot let you race, Sammy. That is final," Claire said. "There is no room for discussion. The answer is no."

"It's not fair," Sam said, then turned and clomped off upstairs in his dad's too-big shoes, carrying a couple of trophies. Claire followed with more of Big Sam's racing memorabilia from the trunk. It took them several trips to haul everything upstairs.

Sam never made it over to Chloe's that evening. He spent the entire night arranging, re-arranging, and running his hands over his father's racing gear and trophies.

When it was finally bedtime, he snuggled in, turned on his bedside lamp, and started to read all the clippings in the envelope.

Sam read every single newspaper story, every headline, looked at every picture. It was 3 o'clock in the morning before he turned out his light to go to sleep.

"Dear God," Sam prayed, "I want to be a drag racer like my dad. Please make mom let me."

CHAPTER 39
Letter

George and Kay Walton were sitting at their kitchen table discussing George's reunion with the McCormick family. George told his wife how terrible he felt about all the years he had avoided them.

"Sammy looks so much like his dad. It's really difficult to look at him, and at the same time I can't seem to look at him enough. Poor kid. Claire kept Big Sam's racing past hidden from him. Sammy has just now discovered all of this about his dad's life, and he now thinks he wants to learn to race."

"That's great," Kay said.

"Not really. You know, Claire lived in a state of perpetual terror over the thought of Big Sam crashing, and now she won't hear of Sammy racing. She didn't even want him to know about Big Sam's racing career, but, like I said, Sammy found out by accident. Wasn't anything Claire could do about that."

"Do you think Claire will change her mind?"

"It doesn't look that way. Roy said she's adamant. If you think back, she never would even go to the drag strip when her husband raced. It's odd since drag racing wasn't what killed Big Sam. Her fear is unfounded, but it's real to her. She won't discuss it."

"I'll be right back," Kay said.

George sipped coffee while his wife disappeared into their home office. She opened a closet and grabbed the stepstool, which she used to reach the top shelf. After rummaging a bit, Kay found the box she was looking for and pulled it down.

Back in the kitchen, she sorted through the items in the box until she came to a small, unopened package.

"What's that?" George asked.

"You mean you really don't know?"

"No."

"It's that package from Big Sam."

"What package?"

"George, you're telling me you don't remember?"

"I don't know what you're talking about. What is that?"

"It's the package from Big Sam, one that he mailed from Iraq just before he was killed. It arrived here after his funeral, and you refused to open it. It's been in this box, hidden in the closet, ever since."

"An unopened parcel from Sam? Oh God. I'd forgotten about it. Should I open it?"

"Well, it's been six years so I'd say it's way past time."

"I'm not sure I can do this," he said, shaking his head, but he took the small box from his wife's hand and examined the familiar handwriting of his best friend. He used his pocket knife to split the tape that held the parcel closed. Inside he found three items plus a letter, which he held in silence for several minutes. Then he slipped his thumb under the flap, unsealed the envelope, opened the folded page, and read the letter aloud so that Kay could hear it.

"*Hey Georgie*," the letter began, and this made George smile. No one except Big Sam ever called him "Georgie." It had started as a joke when they were kids, and it stuck, with Big Sam anyway. George hated the nickname, but he never minded when his best friend used it.

"*This letter is probably an unnecessary precaution. I'm planning on coming back home from Iraq. But, just in case the worst happens, there is something on my mind, and I'll need your help with it if I don't make it back.*

"*You know how Claire feels about drag racing. She developed this irrational fear about it. What worries me is if I don't make it back and Sammy grows up and wants to race, like me. If I'm not there, I just know Claire will put her foot down. I can't believe I'm even thinking this, but for all I know, if I die she might not want to tell Sammy that I ever had anything to do with racing, but surely she wouldn't go that far.*

"*Anyway, Georgie, if I don't come home, I know you'll be a big part of Sammy's life. I want you to be.*"

At this last, George stopped reading. He felt an overwhelming wave of guilt overtake him and tears welled up in his eyes. Kay put her hand on his to reassure him.

"Go on," she said.

"*And if that little guy of mine wants to learn to race when he is old enough, then, Georgie, I'm asking you to intervene with Claire. Show her this letter if you have to. I'm writing this to you instead of her because if I'm not around, someone will need to reason with her. However you do it, tell her this: If Sammy would like to race, I want him to race. Period.*

"*And, one last favor, Georgie—if I am not there to teach him, I want you, with Roy's help, to teach my son to follow his own racing dream as far as he wants to go.*

"Thanks, amigo. I'm sure I'll see you in a few months and none of this will be necessary, but I'm mailing this letter just in case. They shoot live rounds over here, you know, but I'm just too fast for them. Keep your pedal to the metal and your eyes on the finish line." The letter was signed, simply, *"Sam."*

George and Kay sat in silence for quite awhile. Kay finally spoke.

"What will you do, George?"

"I don't know. Here I haven't seen the McCormicks for six years, and now I find out that Sammy wants to race and that Big Sam wanted me to stand up to Claire. I don't see that it's any of my business, especially since I have avoided them for so long."

"Yeah," Kay said. "Good point. Like Claire would pay any attention to you. I mean, even with the letter—Big Sam's gone; it's her decision now."

CHAPTER 40
Conference

Claire pulled up in front of Sam's school, dreading the conference with his teacher. She knew it would be more of the same: Sam was listless, Sam didn't pay attention, Sam was a poor student. Claire didn't know what she could do about it, but the teacher had called, so Claire had come to the school.

Inside, Claire found her way to the library, and there sat Sam's teacher. She felt like running back out the front door and pretending that she'd forgotten the conference, but, of course, she opened the library door and greeted Mrs. Flink.

And to Claire's complete shock and amazement, Mrs. Flink immediately produced a paper, which she handed to Claire. She recognized her son's handwriting, but she was confused when she saw a red "A" at the top of the page.

"I don't understand," Claire said.

"Neither do I," Mrs. Flink said. "I was hoping you could explain."

"What is this?" Claire asked, and the teacher told Claire about the assignment for the students to write something descriptive.

"This paper is perfect," Mrs. Flink said. "I've never known Sam to be so articulate, to show such enthusiasm. I didn't know he was interested in drag racing."

"In what?" Claire said.

"Read the paper yourself," Mrs. Flink suggested.

What she read was a clear description of a race car lining up to race, then of the driver paying attention to the Christmas tree of lights that starts the race, then of the race itself, including reaction time, elapsed time, miles per hour. Claire was stunned. Sam had even beautifully described a junior dragster.

"I don't know what to say," she said to the teacher.

"Well, there's more," Mrs. Flink said. "When Truman got the second chance at his science project, Sam helped him make the presentation to the class. Both boys were amazing, and they held the entire class at full attention. We've never had so many questions about a science project, and I've never seen those two boys as interested in something and as fascinating as they were that day. From my understanding, the discussion continued on the playground."

Claire was silent, then finally managed to say that she was glad to hear this news.

"The reason I called you here, Mrs. McCormick, is to tell you that you were absolutely brilliant in managing to get Sam interested in racing. I sincerely believe this is the one thing that will turn things around for him as nothing else has done all year. He really is like a completely different boy when he is writing about this"—she nodded toward the paper—"or talking about racing. I wish all parents would take such an interest in their children, help them find their true passion."

Mrs. Flink did add, though, that both Sam and Chloe would have detention for three days for skipping school.

"Uh, yes, well, thank you. Thank you so much, Mrs. Flink," Claire said as she excused herself.

Back out in front of the school, sitting in her car, Claire thought she was incapable of driving at that moment. So, for the longest time, she sat there, staring at the street ahead and thinking. Just thinking.

"Good grief," she said, when she finally pulled away from the curb. "Now what?"

CHAPTER 41
Teenagers

Every weekend that they could, Sam and Truman went up to the farm to help Roy and George work on the Chevelle. This particular weekend, the plan was to remove the gas tank so that it could be boiled out. Roy explained to the boys that any time a car sits for a long time it is necessary to have the gas tank boiled out to remove any foul gas or other contamination.

"And, we'll need to clean the fuel line from the tank to the carburetor, too," he said.

In the meantime, the boys knew they were getting closer and closer to being able to go for a ride in the old car.

"Let's go for a walk," Truman said to Sam.

George and Roy were busy disconnecting the fuel line, and there wasn't much for the boys to do, so they took Banjo and headed out. Not surprisingly, they took the short cut they had discovered and wound up at the Atlanta Dragway, where there were two teenage boys hanging out at one of the picnic tables just outside the Dragway.

Sam and Truman walked around outside the strip, which was closed. After that, they sat down at one of the other picnic tables, trying to pretend they weren't listening to the teenagers, who apparently were brothers.

"I'm getting closer," one said. "Pretty soon I'll have enough to buy my own car."

"Yeah, I know. And, remember, I'm saving up, too," said the other one. "I'm gonna ask Uncle Pete if he'll chip in."

"I'm going to race mine," the first teen said.

"Mine'll beat yours any day of the week and twice on Sunday," bragged the other.

And on it went until Truman couldn't stand it anymore. He walked over toward the teenagers.

"We have a car," he said.

"Shut up, kid," said the older teen, whose name was J. L.

"We do," Sam said. "It's at my grandpa's house. My dad used to race it."

"What kind of car?" asked Lloyd, the younger teen.

"Chevelle," Sam and Truman said together.

"Welly, well," said J. L., a tall blond who seemed to wear a permanent smirk. "Where does your grandpa live?"

"Not far," Sam said. "Close to the old dairy."

"Where exactly?"

"Um, well, the next drive toward town from the dairy."

"The Johnson place?" J. L. asked.

"Yeah," Sam said. "Do you know my grandpa?"

"Our dad does," J. L. said. "You two aren't old enough to drive. We could take you for a little ride in your Chevelle. How about that?"

"Well," Sam said, "it's not quite ready yet. We're still working on it."

"When'll it be ready?" asked Lloyd.

"It's close," Truman said. "Mr. Johnson said just a couple more weekends."

"Where do you two live?" J. L. asked.

"In Atlanta, but we come here on weekends to work on the Chevelle," Sam said.

"We're just taking a break now," Truman added.

"You coming up next weekend?" asked J. L.

Truman shrugged. "Don't know."

"Well, maybe we'll see you one of these days," said Lloyd, the shorter and stouter of the two brothers. "Maybe we'll come out to your farm."

"OK," both boys said. "You could see our car."

"Yep," J. L. and Lloyd said. "We'd like that," J. L. added.

As Sam and Truman walked away, the two teenagers high-fived each other.

"Dude," Lloyd said.

J. L. smiled.

CHAPTER 42
Standoff

S am was at the computer in the den, the same place he was every day when Claire got home from work. It had been like that for weeks now. All he did was read about drag racing online. And when he wasn't doing that, he was either listless or restless and angry.

"Dinner's ready," Claire called from the kitchen. She had to call three times before Sam finally showed up at the table. And when he sat down, he took about four bites before declaring he was finished.

"What's wrong?" Claire asked. "Spaghetti's your favorite meal. And you didn't even touch your roll."

"Not hungry."

"I don't believe that. You hardly touched your lunch. Most of it is still in your lunchbox."

"Wasn't hungry."

"Sammy," she said, shaking her head, "racing is dangerous. And that's that. You can go to the drag strip with your grandfather. You can learn to be a mechanic or a crew chief. But you may not race. I will not allow it. Ever. Since you do all this research about drag racing, maybe you can become a sports journalist and write about drag racing."

"I'm going to race," Sam said, as he got up, threw down his napkin, and kicked his chair.

"Come back here now," Claire said. "Apologize, and leave the table properly. You need to get over this fixation about racing."

Sam returned to the table, picked up his napkin, tossed it in the trash can, and pushed his chair in properly.

"I'm sorry," he said, without meaning it. "But I'm going to race. I am."

Sam returned to the computer, typed in the URL for the National Hot Rod Association, and resumed reading. Claire called Essie and went over the racing problem for the umpteenth time.

"You need to relent," Essie told her daughter. "Racing is in his blood. That's just a fact of life. Let George and Roy teach him to do it correctly. It will be fine. You're going to lose this battle."

"I can't do that. I can't stand by and let my boy take up a dangerous sport that could get him killed. I can't have both a husband and a son killed."

"Racing didn't kill your husband, Claire."

"No, but it could have. The answer is no. Sammy will never race."

"You're going to live to regret this," Essie said. "Mark my word."

CHAPTER 43
Big Day

At long last, Truman and Sam—with considerable help from George and Roy—had their Chevelle ready to crank up and drive. The two boys had barely been able to sleep for the last few nights, just imagining that "their" car was ready to hit the road.

They were on the way out to the farm now. Claire was driving, and Kathleen, Chloe, and Uncle Phil also had come along for the big day. Truman's mom had to work or she would have come with them.

The mood was festive when they arrived. Essie had made cupcakes, lemonade, and coffee, and they all had a snack before walking out to the barn together. Kathleen, Claire, and Essie carried their digital cameras.

Banjo arrived at the barn first and greeted them all with his most eager barking.

Not wanting to damage even the bumper of the Chevelle, Essie—in the tradition of christening and launching new ships—broke a bottle of inexpensive champagne on the barn door. Then, the adults toasted each other with champagne poured from another bottle while the kids toasted with sparkling white grape juice.

Finally, it was time for the Chevelle to strut her stuff.

George took the driver's seat, Roy rode shotgun. Sam, Truman, and Chloe climbed into the back. The Chevelle started on the first try.

"Woo-hoo," yelled Sam.

"Yeah, hot dog," said Truman.

George slipped the car into first gear and off they went.

Both Truman and Sam knew they had never felt prouder of anything they'd ever done in their entire lives. Their smiles were about to break their faces.

"This is so cool," Chloe said. "Way to go."

It was no surprise to anyone when George drove over to the drag strip. There was an event that evening, and several people already had arrived. Even though the parking lot was filling up, George drove up near the entrance for the race cars and got out, explaining he wanted to talk to a few friends. He and Roy went off together. The kids stayed near the Chevelle, as people kept stopping by to admire it.

"Well, lookie here," said a voice that Truman and Sam recognized. It was J. L., one of the teenage brothers they had met at the drag strip a few weeks ago.

"See," Truman said. "I told you. We have a car."

"Nice," cooed J. L. "Real nice."

He walked all around the Chevelle, admiring it. Then he popped the hood to examine the engine.

"Nice," he said again.

Truman and Sam followed him around, proud to show off their accomplishments.

"We put in the spark plugs ourselves," Sam said.

"And at first Sam's grandpa turned it with a breaker bar," Truman said.

"Uh-huh," J. L. said.

Chloe took an instinctive dislike to J. L., who disappeared into the crowd before George and Roy returned.

After leaving the drag strip, the five of them drove around for awhile longer, then went back to the farm, where Essie had promised a dinner fit for champions. She had even ordered a cake from the bakery with a likeness of the Chevelle painted in black frosting on the top layer.

After dinner, Claire, Kathleen, and Phil headed back to Atlanta; the kids decided to sleep over. Roy would drive them home tomorrow.

Before going to sleep, Truman and Sam walked out to the barn one more time to admire their hot car.

CHAPTER 44
Trouble

Chloe was asleep before the boys started out to the barn as were Roy and Essie. Even Banjo was down for the night.

Truman and Sam made their way out to the barn with a flashlight and were shocked, as they got closer, to hear voices. They turned off the flashlight, stopped, and listened. The boys were scared and wanted to run back to the house, but they stayed.

"No," one voice said. "I think it's over here."

"No, no, I've done this before. Let me try," said another voice, this one more familiar to Truman and Sam.

"It's those brothers," Sam whispered.

"What are they doing?" Truman whispered back.

"Let's look," Sam said, and the boys walked as slowly and quietly as they could to the barn.

The driver's door to the Chevelle was open, and J. L. was bent down—half in half out—of the car. All Truman and Sam could see were his legs.

"He's trying to hot-wire our car," Truman whispered to Sam, who had had enough.

"Hey," Sam shouted. "What do you think you're doing? Get out of here."

"Ouch," J. L. bumped his head on the steering wheel when he raised up to see Truman and Sam standing there.

"Oh," he said all nice and syrupy, "hey boys."

"Get out of here," Truman said.

"Now guys," said Lloyd. "We were just looking things over."

"You were not," Truman said. "You were trying to hot-wire the car and steal it."

"Not steal it," said J. L., "just borrow it. We'll bring it back."

"You'd better beat it," Sam said, "before I go get Pop. My grandma is best friends with the sheriff."

"Hold on," said J. L. "How would you boys like to race your car? That's why we wanted to borrow it."

"Huh?" Truman and Sam said at the same time.

"There's a street race up the road tonight. The winner gets real money. You wanna go?" asked Lloyd.

"Uh," Sam said.

"Sure," Truman said.

"Truman!" Sam said. "We can't do that."

"Sam," Truman whispered. "Come on. This'll be fun. Your mom won't let you race. We can't drive. Let's see what it's like. Nothing can happen. Everybody's asleep in there. No one will ever know. Just once. Let's do it."

"But… " Sam said.

"C'mon," Truman said. "The sooner we go, the quicker we get back."

Reluctantly, Sam agreed and went to get the spare key from the workbench. J. L. and Lloyd got into the front seat; Sam and Truman climbed into the back. As they pulled out of the farm's drive onto the main road, Sam was nervous and a little scared, but also very excited. He was finally going to race. And this was the night.

Inside, Roy awoke to the roar of an engine, but he quickly fell back to sleep.

After about twenty minutes, they arrived at a desolate stretch of old road somewhere out in the country. Sam and Truman had no idea where they were. There were about a dozen teenagers gathered around an old car. Sam and Truman stayed near the Chevelle while the teenagers all talked among themselves.

"I told you," J. L. said to the gathered group of boys. "Here's our car. Who's going to race us?"

"I am," said one of the kids from the crowd. "No way you're winning with that old buggy."

"We'll find out, won't we," said J. L. as the older boys continued talking among themselves, picking which car they thought would win.

Sam, meanwhile, whispered to Truman that they needed to hide in the trunk. He knew the older boys wouldn't let them stay in the backseat during the race.

"We don't have the key," Truman said.

"I always keep one in my pocket," Sam said. "I got it from Pop, and he lets me keep it."

Making sure the older boys didn't see them, Sam and Truman climbed into the Chevelle's trunk and pulled the lid down with a small piece of rope that had been tied on the inside of the lid.

"Shh," Sam said. "We have to be quiet or they'll make us get out."

Finally, out on the road, someone came up with a piece of chalk and marked a starting line and then a finish line about a quarter mile up the stretch of road. Since it was dark, several teens lined up on either side of the finish line, so it would be clear for the drivers to see where it was. The two cars pulled into place, side by side. In the trunk, both Truman and Sam were close to peeing in their pants from fear and excitement. This wasn't exactly where they wanted to be for their first race, but it would have to do.

Nobody noticed that the two younger boys were missing.

Finally, a boy standing beside the road held up both of his arms and counted down. "Three, two, one," he shouted as he suddenly lowered his arms. With a roar, the two cars took off into the darkness.

CHAPTER 45
Aftermath

Essie awoke to a knock at the door. It was 2 a.m.

"Roy," she said, shaking her husband. "Get up. Someone's at the door."

"What?"

"The door. Someone's knocking at the door."

"What time is it?"

"Just get up and see who it is," Essie said.

Roy pulled on his trousers, Essie found her bathrobe, and both answered the door together to find Sheriff Billy Humphries standing there.

"Billy?" Roy said.

"Essie, Roy," the sheriff said, lowering his head and raising his shoulders. "I have bad news. Sammy and Truman have been in an accident. You'd better get dressed and come with me."

"An accident?" Essie said. "No, they're asleep."

"No, Essie," the sheriff said. "They're at the hospital."

"But how?" Roy said.

"Oh, Roy," said Essie, finally coming to her senses. "Let's just get Chloe and go. Billy, we'll be there in ten minutes."

As they quickly dressed and got Chloe to do the same, Roy and Essie decided not to call Claire until they knew what was going on.

The short drive to the hospital felt like an hour. Roy parked at the emergency entrance, and the three of them ran inside where they found Billy waiting.

"Back here," he said, and they followed him.

Truman and Sam were in the same cubicle, stretched out on separate beds, where a doctor was examining Sam.

When he saw his grandparents, he started to cry.

"How bad are they?" Essie asked the doctor.

"Well," said the doctor. "Truman here has cracked his collar bone. Sammy has dislocated his shoulder and broken his nose. They'll be fine though."

Essie and Roy stepped out to speak with Sheriff Humphries. Chloe stayed with Truman and Sam.

"Billy," Essie said, "where did this happen? Where were they? How did you find them?"

The sheriff explained about the illegal street race and what he had been able to piece together about J. L. and Lloyd, who also were in the emergency room.

"The Chevelle is in good condition," the sheriff explained. "The two teenagers lost control of it. I don't have to tell you, Roy, how powerful that old muscle car is."

"Sure don't," Roy said. "How did the teens get the car? Oh, go on, we'll get to that."

"The Chevelle spun around, and the older boys hadn't bothered with the seat belts so they got tossed around inside the car. Truman and Sammy had hidden in the trunk."

"How did they even end up there? At an illegal street race, I mean," Essie said.

"In a minute, Essie," the sheriff said. "Let me finish. When the car spun out, the two of them rolled around in the trunk where the jack, among other things, was not tied down."

"Good heavens," Essie said. "I've got to call Claire, but first tell me how all this came about."

"J. L. and Lloyd York, that's the two older boys—apparently they showed up at your farm to, um, 'borrow' the Chevelle, and Sammy and Truman caught them. Then the teenagers convinced Sammy and Truman to go with them to race the Chevelle."

"How did Sammy and Truman even know these York boys?" Essie asked, then added, "Oh never mind, I have to call my daughter."

Roy went back to get the rest of the story from Sam and Truman.

CHAPTER 46
The Reckoning

George Walton and Kirby were working overtime to get George's Pro Stock Camaro back in fighting form, and many nights—especially weekend nights—found them in George's garage 'til after midnight. This particular night, as they worked, they were listening to George's police scanner when they picked up something about an illegal street race and thought they caught Roy Johnson's name.

George called the sheriff's office and learned enough to realize that he needed to go to the hospital down in Commerce. Before he left, some sixth sense told him to grab the letter from Big Sam.

George had already arrived and was at the hospital with Essie, Roy, and Chloe when Claire showed up, having driven from Atlanta as fast as she dared.

"What have I done?" Claire said to her parents and to George after she checked on Sam and Truman. "I never should have let it get this far. I knew I never should have let you take him to the drag strip, Dad. It's my fault."

"No, Claire," Roy said. "I think you've got it wrong. What you should have done is let George and me teach the boys how to race safely. You should have let them become junior racers and learn to race in safe conditions at the drag strip. I should have made you do that."

"But," Claire started, until her mother interrupted her.

"He's right," Essie said. "Sammy would never have done this if he weren't so bound and determined to race. You can't stop the boy from living, Claire. You have to let him be who he is. And he is Sam McCormick's son. Racing is in his blood, and you know it."

"Um," George said, and they all turned to look at him. "Claire, I think it's time to show you something." George pulled the letter from Big Sam out of his pocket and handed it to Claire.

"I didn't even remember ever receiving it," George said. "I couldn't bear to read it when it arrived shortly after we buried my best buddy. But Kay kept it, and after I ran into Roy and Sammy at the drag strip, she pulled it out, and I read it for the first time."

Claire looked at the letter in her hand.

"I'm sorry, Claire," George added. "I wasn't going to show it to you, but now I think you should see it."

With curiosity high, everyone remained silent while Claire read her husband's wish—that he wanted his son to be able to race if that's what Sammy wanted to do. With a troubled look on her face, she passed the letter to Roy and Essie, who read it together.

"George," Claire said. "I can't believe this. You mean you never read this yourself before a few weeks ago?"

"That's right," George said. "And after I read it, I didn't think I had any right to show it to you since I avoided you and Sammy all these years. Maybe if I had, tonight would never have happened."

"No, George," Claire said, "it's not your fault." Claire turned to leave, but stopped and turned around. "Mom, would you call Tammy and give her an update? I told her we would. I'm going to check on the boys."

"Well," Roy said to George. "I don't know if this helps or hurts Sammy's chances of ever getting to race."

"Me, neither," George answered. "But I have an idea."

CHAPTER 47

Surprise

Sam and Truman had spent several weeks recuperating, and both were doing well enough so Claire was taking them out to the farm on a Saturday morning. Truman's mom was in the car with them, and following in Kathleen's Honda were Kathleen, Chloe, and Uncle Phil.

George and Kay Walton were driving to the farm from their home in Athens. Sheriff Humphries was going to be there, too.

Unbeknownst to the kids, it was going to be a big day in Commerce.

Even J. L. and Lloyd were there, hiding in the barn.

When Claire pulled up at the farm and Sam saw balloons out front, he asked, "What's going on?"

"Oh," said Claire, crossing her fingers behind her back because she was about to tell a lie, "we're just celebrating that you and Truman are doing well."

Essie had tables and chairs set up out back, and there were refreshments. After everyone got something to eat and drink, Roy stood up, tapped a spoon against his glass, and asked for everyone's attention.

"Um," he said. "First of all, Essie and I are so glad all of you could come to celebrate that Sammy and Truman are just about all healed up. So, let's drink a toast to Sammy and Truman."

Everyone raised their glasses and sipped either iced tea or lemonade.

"And now," Roy said. "We're going to have a little ceremony. I would like to introduce our first speaker—my daughter, Claire."

Claire stood up.

"Sammy," Claire said, "while you have been recuperating, I have been thinking. And thinking. And praying. And talking to George. And talking to Mom and Dad. Son, just before your dad was killed, he sent George here a letter from Iraq. And in that letter, Big Sam told George that if you really, really wanted to race when you got older, he wanted you to be able to follow your dream."

Sam sucked in his breath. Chloe and Truman, their eyes wide, turned to look at Sam, who was afraid to make a sound for fear he would spoil the moment. He could not believe what he was hearing.

Claire continued. "Your dad knew better than to tell me because he knew how I felt about racing. But, son, I cannot ignore a request that Big Sam made before he died, so I have decided... to let you race."

At this, Sam, Truman, and Chloe erupted into clapping and squeals of delight.

"I can't believe it," Sam said to his two friends.

After they calmed down, Claire resumed. "Now, after I made that decision, it occurred to me that Truman and Chloe might also like to race, so I took it up with Kathleen and Tammy, and they both agreed and said it would be fine with them."

Chloe and Truman high-fived each other.

"Wow," Chloe said.

"But," Claire continued, "that presented something of a problem."

The kids suddenly looked apprehensive.

"I can't afford a race car or the equipment that goes with it. Neither can Tammy. Neither can Kathleen."

The kids now looked stricken.

"Which brings us to George's part of the ceremony. Take it away, George."

George stood up as Claire sat down.

"At the hospital, the night you boys were injured," George said, "I had an idea. I thought that if Claire would ever agree to let Sammy race then maybe I knew a way to buy a race car. At the time, I was thinking only of Sammy. It hadn't occurred to me that Truman and Chloe might also want to race.

"So, I came out here one day and talked to Roy. He liked my idea, which was this: If we could sell that Chevelle, it would surely bring enough money to buy Sammy a real junior dragster and all the equipment he would need."

"Sell the Chevelle?" Sam said. "No!"

"No way," Truman chimed in.

"Hear me out," George said. "So I started checking around. And in the meantime, Claire told me about Truman and Chloe being in on the deal, too. The old Chevelle is a valuable classic, so I didn't think the additional two kids would be a problem, but I wasn't sure. And this brings me to our next speaker. I would like to introduce Mr. Randall York."

The kids had no idea who this man was.

He stood up—a tall, distinguished-looking gentleman in a suit.

"I know most of you don't know me, but you know my boys, Lloyd and J. L.," Mr. York said. "And you know that they are the two who actually caused the accident."

Sam and Truman couldn't imagine why Lloyd and J. L.'s father was at the farm.

Mr. York explained. "I work with a friend of George's—someone you folks might know. His name is Kirby. And Roy and I also have been acquaintances for many years. Anyway, at work one day, Kirby told me that a friend of his was trying to sell a 1966 Chevelle. This caught my ear because of my sons and the accident so I started asking questions, and I found out that this is the same Chevelle my sons almost stole and nearly wrecked.

"And, to tell you the truth," he said with a long sigh, "I felt a little guilty about what those boys of mine did. If I had been paying more attention, as their father, I would have bought them a car, maybe taught them to race legally, and this would never have happened. Now, don't get me wrong, they've been punished for what they did—both by me and by the sheriff here.

"Anyway, I decided it was the least I could do to pay top dollar for the Chevelle and buy it for my sons. We hope that you boys will be satisfied."

At this, Mr. York whistled, and everyone turned around to see the Chevelle being driven out of the barn, with J. L. behind the wheel and Lloyd beside him.

As they drove up to the gathering, Truman and Sam approached the car tentatively. Then the older boys apologized.

George asked Truman and Sam if they were OK with J. L. and Lloyd owning the Chevelle.

"Could we ride in it sometimes?" Sam asked.

"Sure thing," J. L. answered. He seemed nicer now than he had before the illegal street race that landed all four boys in the hospital.

Lloyd was friendlier, too. He nodded. "We'd never have known about it if it weren't for you guys."

When things quieted down, Sam asked, "Are we going to get race cars?"

At this, George made a call on his cell phone, and minutes later Kirby drove up, pulling a large trailer.

Everybody walked over to where Kirby had parked. He and George motioned everyone to the back of the trailer. When Kirby opened the huge trailer door, everyone was stunned. There sat three of the most fantastical half-scale dragsters any of them had ever seen.

The three junior dragsters were brand new, their fiberglass bodies and steel frames gleaming. Even their 5 horsepower Briggs & Stratton engines sparkled. With each of them nearly sixteen feet long, they filled up the trailer.

Chloe jumped into the arms of a surprised George. Sam tried to keep from crying, but his eyes filled up when he looked at Pop. Claire didn't even try to hold back her tears, which were rolling down her cheeks and dropping onto her blouse. For his part, Truman went completely silent. Pop put his right arm around Essie and his left arm around his daughter.

Phil had a grin that stretched from ear to ear. Standing next to her brother, Kathleen said, "I'm not sure I've ever seen Chloe quite so excited."

Tammy, who could not believe how her son's life had turned around, closed her eyes briefly and said a silent prayer of thanks.

Kirby and Sheriff Humphries looked on, laughing and chatting with the Yorks while Kay snapped photos and the kids began examining their new cars.

Chloe's car was purple and hot pink with the image of a dolphin on both sides. Balanced on the dolphin's nose was a ball proclaiming: "Chloe: Smart Fish."

Suddenly, she yelled, "I love it. I love it," at the top of her lungs then hopped into the trailer.

For Truman's car, Tammy had chosen a dragon motif. The car was painted deep green, with, of course, lots of oranges, reds, and yellows for the flames coming out of the dragon's mouth. Truman's name was swirled into the fire.

Truman, who had turned very quiet, was simply awestruck. He climbed into the trailer, squatted down, and ran his hands along the exterior of his car. Never could Truman—the one-time class bully—have imagined such a day.

Finally, in honor of Big Sam, Claire had chosen a desert camouflage pattern for Sam's car. And, in addition to his dad's number, 3183—which George got permission from the National Hot Rod Association for Sam to use—the words on Sam's car read, "Thanks, Dad. Sam McCormick Jr."

After a while, George said. "Let's get these cars out of here. We got to get started on some serious driving lessons."

CHAPTER 48

Practice

Once on the drag strip, George pushed Chloe's purple and pink car into the staging lane. Decked out in her hot pink fire suit, fireproof shoes, and purple helmet, she was buckled in and ready for her first solo run down the lane. Like Sam and Truman, Chloe already had made a couple of slow runs with Kirby and Roy posted up ahead to stop her in case of problems. But she had no problems. Chloe drove like a natural champ.

The three kids, along with George, Kirby, and Roy, had spent several days at the farm learning safety and the basics. Today, they were finally practicing at the drag strip.

The starter—today it was Roy—gave the thumbs up, and George fired Chloe's engine.

She rolled up through the water box and executed a burnout—spinning her back tires to heat them up and make them sticky. George, standing just behind Chloe at her car's engine, handled last-minute tuning. He adjusted the rpms and checked the engine temperature.

Chloe moved slowly and slightly forward and saw the small amber bulbs on top of the Christmas tree light up. Her heart began pounding. Truman and Sam, watching from just beside her, both took deep breaths. She was prestaged. Now Chloe moved ever so slightly forward again, and the second row of small twin amber bulbs lit up. Chloe was staged. Her heart beat harder.

Both Truman and Sam held their breath.

Chloe's eyes were fixed on the Christmas tree. She saw the top large amber bulb light up, then the middle large amber bulb. Chloe was focused like a laser now. As she saw the bottom amber bulb light up, Chloe flew off the starting line.

Her engine roared and the thrust pushed her back into her seat. Chloe's grasp on the steering wheel was so intense that underneath her safety gloves her knuckles were turning white. The acceleration of the car was exhilarating. She could feel her heart pounding, but she was totally focused on keeping the dragster steady in the center of her lane, and she could see the finish line drawing closer. In what seemed like a heartbeat, but was really more like twelve seconds, Chloe had completed her one-eighth-mile run.

Chloe was ecstatic; she had never experienced a feeling like this. When she turned her car to the left off the lane and saw George there in his golf cart, ready to pick her up and tow her car back up to where the others were waiting, she broke into a huge grin.

When she climbed out of the car her legs were shaking. It took a few seconds for her to catch her breath. She had never been so thrilled by anything in all her life. Her heart felt like it might pop out of her chest. She had chill bumps all down her back.

"Oh, Mr. Walton," she said, "that was unbelievable."

George reached over with one arm and gave her a big hug. "I know," he said. "And you were perfect."

When they got back down to the starting line, Kirby had pushed Sam's car into position. Chloe joined Truman on the sideline to watch Sam's first run down the lane.

Sam was nervous. His mind was everywhere. Suddenly it seemed he couldn't remember anything he'd learned.

When Roy gave the signal, Kirby started Sam's car. Then, as Chloe had done, Sam rolled into the water box and did his burnout. So far, so good. Kirby made the final adjustments—checking the tune on the carburetor and making sure the engine temperature was ready for racing. Then Sam rolled forward a tiny bit and saw the top bulbs on the Christmas tree light up. Forward a little more and he saw the second set of bulbs light up.

Then, one, two, three—the larger amber bulbs lit up. Sam took off... and he red-lighted. He had misjudged and taken off too soon. The green light hadn't lit up yet. He realized that in a race, this would disqualify him. But for practice, he was allowed to complete his pass down the eighth-mile. His elapsed time would count.

Sam tried twice more and red-lighted again and again. He was completely exasperated.

"Let's give Truman a shot," George finally suggested, "and let you rest. You're just too excited, Sam. You know how to do this."

Dejected, Sam nodded in agreement.

Truman made it through prestaging and staging just fine, and his reaction time was perfect, but—just like Sam—in a real race he would have been disqualified. Truman drove quicker than what junior dragster rules allowed for his age group. They call this breaking out, and Truman kept doing it. George and Roy discussed it and decided they needed to adjust the throttle to slow Truman's car down a bit.

And George thought that Sam, in particular, needed a break.

At the Dairy Queen over ice cream cones, Chloe—acting on George's secret suggestion to her—got the boys to talking about things other than racing. Then they headed back to the drag strip.

It took three more tries for Sam finally to stop red-lighting. The throttle adjustment helped Truman slow down, though not quite enough.

They had two more weeks of practice before they would actually race for the first time.

"Don't you worry, kids," George assured them. "You'll be ready."

CHAPTER 49
Big Day

Essie and Roy had a full house. Tomorrow was the first real race for Sam, Chloe, and Truman, and everybody was going to be there: Kathleen, Uncle Phil, Claire, Tammy, the kids, and Banjo were spending the night. George and Kirby would be there tomorrow, and even Sheriff Humphries vowed to show up.

"What if I red-light?" Sam asked.

"Stop thinking about it or you will," Chloe advised. "And Truman, remember to pedal if you need to so you don't get disqualified for breaking out." The kids had learned that "pedaling" was a method for slowing down to avoid breaking out.

Claire rolled her eyes at her dad. She couldn't believe that her son and his friends were about to drag race for real.

"Sammy," she said, "I'm sure your father's spirit will be riding with you in that car tomorrow. You will not red-light; you'll be perfect. You may not win, but you'll make a perfect run with no mistakes."

Essie smiled at her daughter.

"Truman, I'm not sure I can watch," Tammy said. "But for gosh sakes, be careful."

"Oh, Mom," he said, shrugging his shoulders.

Kathleen had already been told that Chloe was a natural, so she said nothing to her daughter. She just gave her a wink.

"I know I'll red-light," Sam said.

"Oh, stop it," Chloe said.

Since Uncle Phil could tell that tensions were rising, he broke out his banjo and performed a little concert—*Foggy Mountain Breakdown*—right there in Essie and Roy's den. Everybody went to bed relaxed and humming.

The next morning, however, was a different story. Sam felt out of sorts and short-tempered. Truman was quiet and withdrawn. Of the three kids, only

Chloe showed her usual spunk. She was, in fact, so bubbly that Sam wanted to shut her up somehow. Instead, he went out to toss a ball with Banjo.

But he couldn't find his dog anywhere. Then he remembered that, last night, in all his worry about the race he had forgotten to bring him in for the night.

"Banjo! Here Banjo!" Sam called, but the dog did not come.

Sam took off running, forgetting to tell anybody that Banjo was missing or that he was going to search for him.

Inside, after pancakes and kitchen clean-up, as everybody was getting ready to load up into separate cars and trucks and head to the Atlanta Dragway, they realized Sam was nowhere to be found.

Chloe and Truman searched out by the old barn. Claire looked through the house, calling his name. Everyone else struck out in various directions, calling for Sam—who didn't answer.

When everyone was back at the house and frantic that Sam had disappeared, Claire convinced them they should head on over to the drag strip. The last thing she wanted was for Chloe and Truman to miss the race. She would stay back and wait for Sam and Banjo to return. By now, they had figured out that Sam must have gone looking for Banjo because no one remembered seeing the dog this morning.

On arriving at the drag strip, Chloe and Truman were overwhelmed. Kids and their parents were everywhere. The parking lot was jammed with trailers, golf carts, race cars.

This was a special day. In celebration of an important anniversary, the drag strip was allowing the kids to race on the same day as the national pro event. The air seemed to vibrate with excitement.

Crew members for the pros were riding around on scooters, golf carts, and ATVs, taking fuel jugs to the fueling center or hauling worn-out slicks (tires) to supplier tents to get new ones. Crews were firing the nitro engines to make sure they were working correctly, and that noise is akin to having a jet plane fly over at treetop level. Maybe it's louder. Fans were roaming the pits, drivers were signing autographs.

Truman got to feeling a little cocky. Chloe jumped right in and started talking to the other junior racers. Several girls came over to admire and coo over her pink and purple car.

After nearly an hour, Sam still had not appeared.

"Chloe, Truman," George said, "We really need to get you two on over to the staging area."

"But we can't race without Sam," Chloe said.

"No," Truman agreed. "We can't do it."

"Kids," George said, "we've got to trust that Sam will show up, but you can't miss the race. Sam wouldn't want that. Try not to worry. He'll be here."

"I'll go over to the staging area," Chloe declared, "but I'm not racing if Sam's not racing."

"Me, neither," Truman said.

Exasperated, George took Chloe and her car over to the staging area. Kirby took Truman and his car. Roy took Sam's car to the staging area—even though, so far, there was no Sam to drive it.

Inside the staging area, the moms were helping their kids into their fire suits and fastening their helmets. Kid brothers and sisters were getting in the way. Dads were making adjustments to their children's cars. It all looked chaotic, but everyone seemed both relaxed and excited.

George explained again to Chloe and Truman about what was called the "Qualifier Shootout," which would determine how they would be placed on the "ladder" for Round One of the race.

"Doesn't matter," Chloe said, "we're not going without Sam."

George looked at his watch and realized it was nearly time for qualifying to begin.

"Where's Sam?" Chloe pleaded to no one in particular.

All of a sudden, the Qualifier Shootout began. The reaction times—how quickly the drivers left the starting line once the Christmas tree turned green—would decide their placement in the first round.

Just as Chloe was about to refuse to participate, she heard a dog barking. Chloe leapt up out of her car, looked around, and spotted Banjo—and Sam, who was running at top speed to the staging area. Claire was right behind him with his fire suit, helmet, and shoes.

"Hurry, Sam, hurry," Truman yelled, finally getting into his own car. And so began the Qualifier Shootout. Sam had made it just in time.

When all the junior racers were done, Sam, Chloe, and Truman gathered with the other kids to look at the posted results in order to learn what their reaction times had been. Based on these times, they all knew who they would race against in Round One, as well as the order of all the pairings.

They returned to the staging area to get ready to race.

When it was Chloe's turn, she heard her name: "Chloe Mullin, in the Summit lane, with a nine point nine zero dial-in," came the announcer's voice over the loud speaker. She had improved her elapsed time since that first day of practice.

"That's me," she thought. "Better get moving."

Chloe slid down into her seat and under the roll cage, and George pushed her forward. The nine point nine zero dial-in the announcer had referred to was the time Chloe had predicted it would take her to make her pass down the one-eighth mile lane for this particular race. Nine and nine-tenths seconds.

"Here we go," Chloe said.

CHAPTER 50
Flashback

Truman, alas, after all of his excitement and preparation, had been eliminated. True to his previous experience, he went quicker than allowed in the second round, so he was done for the day. But he was in good spirits about it, cheering on Sam and Chloe, telling them he was sure they could keep going, maybe even win.

In the first round, Sam raced against a boy named Jason, who had a poor reaction time. Sam, on the other hand, had an excellent reaction time and therefore won.

Chloe, in her first round, was up against a girl, Caitlin. Both of them had good reaction times, and the race was close.

As the two girls approached the finish line, Chloe could see Caitlin's dragster out of the corner of her eye. It looked like they were neck and neck.

"You're good, Caitlin," Chloe said right before she crossed the finish line a split second ahead of her opponent.

"But not as good as me," Chloe whispered to herself as she slowed her car down and broke into a big smile.

In his second round, Sam raced against a boy who drove too quickly and, like Truman, was disqualified.

"Hey, good race," Sam said to the other boy when he saw him a few minutes later.

Chloe had a close second round against a boy named Michael, but her reaction time was better, so she won.

After that round, when she got back up near the staging area, one of the older junior racers, a boy about a year older than Chloe, approached her.

"Hey, you really chopped down the Christmas tree," the boy said, flashing Chloe a smile before he walked away.

Caitlin overheard. "Chloe," she said. "Oh my gosh. Do you know who that was?"

"Who? That boy?" Chloe answered. "No. Who?"

"Jarrett Cooper," Caitlin said, patting her heart. "Everyone has a crush on him, and he never talks to girls."

"Oh," Chloe said. She was still trying to figure out what Jarrett Cooper meant.

When George appeared, she asked.

"He meant that you had a good reaction time," George said.

"I think he likes you," said Caitlin.

Chloe blushed, and just then Sam appeared.

"Who was that?" he asked, turning around to look for Jarrett as he disappeared into the crowd.

"Just a boy," Chloe said.

"Ha!" said Caitlin.

George and Roy told Chloe and Sam it was time to get into their dragsters and get ready for another pass—against each other.

It was the moment Truman was dreading. He couldn't believe Sam and Chloe would be racing against each other. Truman had seen the pairing when the results of the last round had been posted. He hoped somehow he had read it wrong.

Truman had trouble deciding whether to watch or go get a Coke. He stayed.

Inside their cars, ready to prestage, Sam and Chloe couldn't believe it either. On their first day of real racing they would face each other.

"I don't want to beat Chloe," Sam was thinking.

"Should I let Sam win?" Chloe wondered—even though she really knew that she was the better driver.

But they didn't have a lot of time to dwell on their concerns. Before they knew it, they were staged, launched, and racing down their respective lanes, running a close race, until…

"Oh no," Sam screamed. He saw Chloe's car spinning out and flipping over. In a flash, he remembered the story Pop had told him about that night his dad and George raced against each other. That memory was all he needed to make him stop his dragster, hop out of his car, and rush over to help Chloe. He had been halfway down the lane with a good time. He could have won, but Sam remembered hearing that story and, without a second thought, he quit racing and ran instead to help his friend.

"Sammy," Pop had told him, "one night when your dad and George ended up racing against each other turned out to be quite the night.

"Your dad had the better car. His was the car to beat, in fact. Everyone knew it. Both your dad and George had won their first two rounds. In the third round, they raced against each other. Both were making good time, but your dad probably would have been the winner.

"But it wasn't to be because George crashed. And instead of finishing the race, your dad stopped to help his best friend. He did finally cross the finish line and got credit for winning the round, but he wouldn't stay to race in the final round. He went to the hospital with George.

"Your dad turned down a lot of money that night, Sammy. Prestige, too, but his friend was more important to him. It was something to behold.

"George suffered a broken wrist, and—you may have noticed that scar on his face—he got badly cut up and needed a lot of stitches. And maybe that explains a little better to you why George had such a hard time when your dad was killed in Iraq. They truly were the fastest and best of friends."

Sam was the first to get to Chloe. Her car had turned a complete flip and landed upright. He knew better than to move her or even touch her, but he talked to her until the medics arrived, with Truman close on their heels.

"Chloe, talk to me," Sam said, remembering some safety instructions George had given them. "Wasn't this great?"

Chloe looked at Sam and grimaced. "Awesome," she said. "You beat me."

"We weren't done yet," Sam started saying, but he stopped.

"The medics are here," he said instead. "And here comes Truman, too. You're going to be fine," Sam said, sounding braver than he felt.

"Move over, son," came the voice of a medic, who leaned in over Chloe.

"You'll be fine, Chloe," Sam said, letting the medics take over.

"How is she, Sam?" Truman asked, as he ran up, out of breath.

"I don't know," Sam said, "but let's find Pop and get to the hospital."

George appeared.

"Sammy, you need to finish the round, then we'll go to the hospital. You may as well chalk up a win."

His heart wasn't in it, but Sam did cross the finish line, then he left before the next round so he lost his opportunity to be the overall winner that day.

At the hospital, it was determined that Chloe would be fine because her helmet and all the safety features in her car had kept her from serious injury. She would be sore, the doctor said, but nothing was broken. After the doctor dismissed her, with some advice for Kathleen on how to treat the soreness and instructions for Chloe to take it easy for awhile, they all drove back to the farm.

When everyone arrived, Essie made coffee, put out cookies, and fixed hot chocolate for the kids. Everyone was there—Truman, Sam, and Chloe, of course, plus Claire, Kathleen, Tammy, Essie, Roy, George, Kirby, Uncle Phil, and even Sheriff Humphries.

Chloe finally asked Sam, "Why didn't you stay to finish the race? You could have won you know."

Sam didn't know what to say, so George intervened.

"Chloe, Sammy did finish the round, but he didn't stay to finish the race. I think," he said, "that Sammy really did win tonight. Just like his father before him, he did the right thing. He knew that friendship was more important than any race. Later this season and next year," he nodded, "there'll be more races to win. All three of you will be back at the drag strip, winning trophies. No doubt about it. I'll be there, too, soon. Kirby and I almost have my old Camaro back in racing shape."

"But," Roy interrupted, "no race that you ever win will be as important as what you did tonight, Sammy. Tonight you proved that you are for certain your father's son. You knew, just as he knew, that human friendship is always more important than any race between machines. I'm truly proud of you. We all are."

"Uh," George cleared his throat. "Um, Sammy, you remember that letter from your dad?"

"Yeah," Sam said.

"Well, there was something else."

"What?" everyone asked.

"Well," said George, "in the package where he included the letter, Big Sam enclosed some things that he wanted me to give Sammy here when he won his first race. But I think I'll give them to him tonight—if you think that's OK, Claire."

Claire nodded yes.

"Hold on. They're out in my car. I brought them along in case Sammy won tonight."

While George went out to retrieve the gifts, anticipation ran high inside the house.

For his part, Sam couldn't believe that after all this time he was about to receive something from his dad. He had a big lump in his throat.

When George returned, he was carrying three things: Big Sam's college ring, a key ring, and a photograph.

"Here's a picture of your dad and me the very night I crashed," George said, handing the picture to Sam. "As you can see, it was taken at the hospital. He didn't want you to see it before you had won your first race for fear it might frighten you, but he thought you would like to have it. You can see, you look just like him. He was my hero that night. And tonight, I suspect, you are Chloe's hero and always will be."

Sam blushed. So did Chloe.

"Here," George said as he handed a leather key ring to Sam. Affixed to a pear-shaped piece of black leather was a red, white, and blue medallion with the word "Chevelle" on it.

"This is the key ring we used when Roy here finally gave us the keys to the old Chevelle. Your dad didn't think it would be important to you if you ended up with no interest in racing, but if you did race, then he knew you would understand."

Sam took the key ring and stared hard at it as if it were a baseball signed by Chipper Jones, his favorite player on the Atlanta Braves. Then he reached in his pocket and pulled out the key to the Chevelle that he still kept even though the Chevelle had been sold. Now, the old key had the perfect key ring. Sam worked the key onto the Chevelle ring and held it up for everyone to see.

"That's so cool," Truman said.

Essie, Claire, Kathleen—well all of them—were either swallowing hard or dabbing tears from their eyes.

Finally, George handed Sam his dad's college ring—Duke University.

"I always wondered what had become of that," Claire said. "But what… "

"Sammy," George said, "your dad didn't want you to get so caught up in racing that you decided not to go to college. He wanted you to work hard in school and get a good education. And race, too, if that's what you truly want to do. He just didn't want you to sacrifice everything for racing. He told me to give you his college ring as a reminder of that."

Sam stood staring at his father's ring. Slowly, Chloe, Truman, and the others moved closer so they could have a peek, too.

"Look, Mom," Sam said, holding the ring out for Claire, but all she could see was a blur because her eyes were filled with tears.

"Could I go to Duke, too?" Sam asked Claire, who broke into a huge smile. It was the first time she could remember Sam ever mentioning that he wanted to go to college.

"Oh, yes," she answered. "If that's what you want, but you have to keep your grades up."

"I will," Sam vowed. "I promise."

While George was sharing these treasures with Sam, Sheriff Humphries had been busy in the kitchen, pouring champagne for the adults and sparkling juice for the kids. He had stopped by the grocery store on his way from the hospital to the farm. Now he passed out the glasses, all filled with something bubbly.

"I'll go first," the sheriff said. "Here's to Chloe, a super trouper, a smart little fish, and a first-class drag racer."

They all raised their glasses and sipped.

"And," announced Roy, "I officially hereby propose a toast of the highest congratulations to Truman, to Sammy, and to Chloe. Finally, they really are official junior racers, born to win."

"And finally," Essie said, "I would like to propose my own toast to my wonderful grandson, for knowing and doing the right thing tonight."

Glasses went up; everybody sipped again.

At last, Sam held up his own glass, took a deep breath, and cleared his throat.

"Um," he said, as everyone went silent. He looked at the framed photograph that Claire had finally taken from her secret orange trunk and had put on full display in Essie's kitchen for the first time tonight. It was an eight-by-ten full color shot of Big Sam, smiling with his flashy green eyes and red hair, with one arm resting on his Trans Am and the other holding his equally red-haired little baby boy.

"I want to propose a toast," Sam said, "with love and respect and honor forever to my greatest hero, my dad. Thank you, Dad—Big Sam. Thank you for everything."

C.J. Carter, a journalist, lives in Blue Ridge, Georgia, with her husband, two dogs, three cats, several fish, and quite a few turtles. She grew up in Sikeston, Mo., and she is an alumnus of the University of Missouri School of Journalism.

WESTGATE ELEMENTARY
LIC